to Jewell and to Willie

HaSk

Table of Contents

Foreword

THE RIVAL LOVERS, written more than 100 years ago by my great-grandfather, William Ferguson Smith, is the story of a young Georgia boy who went away to war in 1863, fell in love and into great adventure and returned to write of his experience. It is a courtly tale of romance that lay lost and forgotten for almost a century.

The recent discovery of the original text has led me through a personal adventure as dramatic and as satisfying as any detective story or buried treasure tale. It began when the Smith family home in Flovilla, Georgia was sold in 1971 after the death of its owner, Alice Smith Thompson, a daughter of William Ferguson Smith. Alice's half-sister, Jewell Gem Smith, disposed of the estate, distributing items of personal interest and sentimental value among many relatives and friends.

I was fortunate to receive a number of old papers, among which were several of William's letters, original notebooks, and early newspapers of Butts County, Georgia—weekly papers which, under various titles, William edited and published for more than thirty years. I had planned someday to document all of the material and donate it to the Georgia State Archives, but in 1973 Doyle Jones, Jr., late editor of the *Jackson Progress-Argus,* as the paper is now called, wrote to my Great-Aunt Jewell for information and ideas for a commemorative centennial issue. She referred Mr. Jones to me, and I began then in earnest to read my old copies for selections he might find appropriate for the special anniversary edition.

Through his versatile writings, I began to know my ancestor as a real and present person—his serious turn of mind, simple tastes, sense of humor and of honor, his strong emotional feelings, his sensitivity and his values. And I began to wish, with my Aunt Jewell, that "a new generation might come to know him, for what his example and inspiration can mean to them."

My curiosity was particularly sparked by a small announcement in the May 24, 1877 issue of the *Butts County Argus:*

The Rival Lovers

A story of the late war between the States, written for the ARGUS by a citizen of this county, will commence in our next issue. The hero of this story was a native of this county, and as this story is facts instead of fiction, we hope it will prove to be of interest to many of our readers who can recall to mind many of the scenes that will be portrayed in this story.

Jewell, the thirteenth born and last remaining of his sixteen children, said she remembered hearing that her father had written a "novel" but she thought it had been lost in a fire that swept the business district of Flovilla in 1907, destroying the building owned by Captain Smith, as he was then called, in which were housed his offices as well as the town's post office. Jewell's younger sister, Willie Ferguson Smith (1895-1969), had tried especially hard to trace the mysterious phantom book, but to no avail, and no one in later generations even knew of its existence. A grandson, Howard Linch, researched William's military record and wrote to his aunts in 1961, "It would be interesting if someone would or could present the whole in a readable form," not knowing his Grandpa himself had already done so. But Grandpa Smith had put all commentary on the war, if not all thought, behind him in later years. Whether from modesty, wisdom, or the disillusionments of Reconstruction, he shared this reticence with many other soldiers in their old age (Palmer), although until the early 1900s, many newspapers carried regular columns of eagerly shared experiences by front line and home front veterans alike. Even William, in spite of his "never being very expansive on the subject" in later years, seemed full of his story at one time, intent on expressing it in various forms, as revealed in his numerous postwar articles and in correspondence with military comrades (*see* Notes 18 and 21).

The newspapers I had custody of were sporadic and non-consecutive; they produced no further evidence of the announced serial. However, not long after her move back to Manchester, Georgia, where she had taught school for many years, Jewell found more papers in a box she had brought from the old home place but had not yet gone through. One tightly rolled bundle revealed twenty-four yellowed newspaper columns, clipped and edited in William's own hand. Here, at last, was the long-lost novel he had promised and printed nearly a century before, written shortly after the Civil War.

My aunt entrusted these chapters to me, and I have carefully copied the story over and edited it as nearly as possible in the way I feel its author would have approved. William himself never calls it a novel, and perhaps by current definition it isn't. He refers to it simply as a "story."

William Ferguson Smith wrote in a different age from our own and his story cannot rightly be understood and enjoyed by modern criteria alone. Although sharing an intensely personal narrative in *The Rival Lovers,* he nevertheless utilizes many of the quaintly decorous literary formulas of his day—rules of formal and often stilted politeness, of flowery description, of sentimental excess. William does not avoid the gory details of war as fastidiously as did many other writers of popular fiction in the last quarter of the nineteenth century, but his dialogues betray a studied loftiness and unreality of speech common to many books of the period, not only war stories. Unlike the strict conventions of Manners, however, spelling and punctuation were little standardized. Grammatical styles, like civilian and military lifestyles, were highly individual, more casual than comformist.

The story is presented here almost exactly as it was written, with the exception of Chapters I, XVII and XXIV, into which I have incorporated certain events and episodes William actually wrote and published as newspaper articles and editorials in later years, or recounted to descendants who have shared them with me. I have taken the liberty of correcting the manuscript slightly, smoothing the text for the ease and convenience of the modern reader without sacrificing authenticity. I have thus eliminated many commas, divided long sentences, supplied specific words and references for vague pronouns and occasional "et ceteras," clarified questionable antecedents and conflicting tenses except where retained for dramatic emphasis or the flavor of the era. Misspellings, phrasing, words, usage, and idioms customary in William's day (even if changed in connotation today) and his own personal idiosyncracies of style, I have retained.

We do not know how closely all portions of the story parallel William's personal experience or how much is fiction and how much merely fictionalized. We do know that some particulars are truly autobiographical: William has stated that it is "facts not fiction" and occasionally lapses into the first-person form of expression. But the identity, if actual, of certain characters—Florence, Captain Winston and others—remains a mystery for the present. Several years have been spent in researching details and characters, for interest and for accuracy, and I am indebted to all who have helped in this effort.

The Rival Lovers is a simple romance, yet it might well be seen on another level as an allegory of patriotism—the story of two ardent but opposing contenders for the fate and future of one beloved America. William loved his state, his Southland, his nation. He condemned no man who he felt truly sought the good of country and of fellow man.

I have tried to be faithful to his original intent and purpose, which I believe was to tell a moving story in his own plain words.

Harriet S. Kelley

Courtesy of Thomas Melvin Rhodes.

W. F. Smith

THE RIVAL LOVERS!

A SOUTHERN STORY OF THE
LATE WAR BETWEEN THE STATES
FOUNDED ON FACT.

The Call to Arms—The Tented Field—The Field
of Carnage—The Prison Wall—The Con-
querers March—A Desolated Home—
A Lost Cause, Etc.

—BY—

WILLIAM FURGERSON SMITH,

AN EX-CONFEDERATE SOLDIER,

INDIAN SPRING, GEORGIA.

PART ONE

The Rival Lovers

To The Soldiers of the Late War

I dedicate this book to you, hoping that you may find in the perusal of its pages something to recall to mind some memorable and interesting events connected with the struggle in which you bore an active part.

You will discover from its wants of embellishment that the writer is wanting in those educational accomplishments necessary to authorship but as the scenes I have attempted to portray [are] so indelibly impressed on your minds, then you will only appreciate it the more to know that the incidents were not sketched from some eminent position with spy glass in hand but were sketched when by your side amid the smoke of battle with stifling heat, and parching thirst . . .

W.F.S.

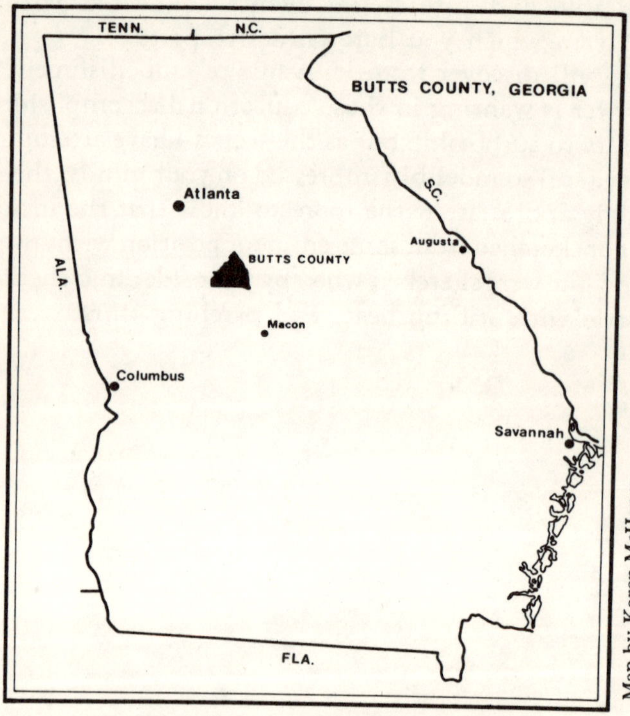

Map by Karen McHaney

Butts County in the Heart of Georgia.

I

The Call to Arms

IN BUTTS COUNTY, Georgia, lived a young man of poor but respectable family, whose name we will call Albert.

Albert, at the breaking out of the late war between the States, was about fourteen years of age, possessing a kindly nature and smooth mild temper, well formed and well developed physically for his age, and termed by his fair acquaintances quite handsome, which made him a great favorite with the fair sex.

While the Southern Confederacy seemed sure of achieving her independence, and the stories of her armies' triumphs were ringing through the land firing anew the determination of every young patriot who had not yet enlisted in his country's defense, Albert determined to hurry to the front and share the glory and imperishable renown which had been won by his young comrades upon the bloody fields of Manassas and Richmond.

Albert possessed, in common with many of his countrymen, a natural taste for the military life, which had been roused into action and cultivated by reading the history of struggles of the colonies against the Mother Country during the Revolutionary war, and we do not exaggerate when we say it was with perfect delight he heard his native State had severed her connection with the Union. His young imagination was all aglow with the determination he had formed to proceed, as soon as he had arrived at the age to gain admittance into the ranks of the army, and to battle for his country. It was in vain that his parents, seconded by the advice of friends, urged that he was too young and weak to undergo the fatigues and exposure of camp life, which they laid before him in all its true colors. A compromise was finally effected by Albert's parents' consenting to allow him to join a battalion of youths for State defense, which was encamped in the city of Macon, and had its permanent headquarters fixed at that point[1] making ready to meet the enemy whenever he appeared upon the soil of the Empire State.

His arrangements for leaving home were soon completed, and on a beautiful morning in September, when the golden rays of an autumn sun were shining through the windows of the old farm house, Albert took an affectionate leave of his loving parents and many kind friends who had assembled to bid him God speed. His mother, with the tears in her eyes, gave him a pocket-sized dictionary and a small Bible which he carried with him always and would read to his comrades seated around the campfire at night. Then throwing her arms about his neck, she tearfully bade him farewell.

He shouldered his knapsack and haversack, which had been filled with clothing and other provisions necessary for his comfort and convenience, by the kindness of his mother, and began his journey to the camps. The distance was not great, but seemed quite long to our hero who only wished he could fly, such was the anxiety of his heart to become a soldier.

Once enlisted, Albert soon learned the routine of camp life

duties, became a great favorite with his comrades on account of his obliging nature, and of his officers by the ardor of his conduct, and the alacrity displayed in performing every duty imposed upon him. Time might have dragged heavily but for the constant drills and public parades which were witnessed by many ladies of all ages, who did all in their power to cheer the soldiers' hearts, and drive away thoughts of home and the despondency consequent upon such thoughts. Besides, the city of Macon has many attractions, being justly celebrated then as now, for its many hansdome private residences, which are surrounded by beautiful gardens that contain almost every shrub and flower which will bloom or thrive in that highly favored climate. Macon also boasts one of the most romantic cemeteries in the United States, and the officers were very indulgent in granting permissions to their young soldiers to visit the city and suburbs which had a very beneficial effect upon their minds and health.

On a quiet afternoon in that enchanting season known as Indian Summer, Albert secured a passport, and wended his way to the beautiful Rose Hill Cemetery,[2] which is the pride of the city and admiration of every visitor. Its situation is upon the banks of the Ocmulgee river that flows past the city, and the romantic spot is filled with many species of natural shrub and tree, from the modest violet which peeps from beneath the grassy carpet, "as if afraid, yet anxious to be seen," to the towering oak and pine with their clinging parasites*, rendering it a place of beauty at all seasons of the year. Indeed many tourists compare it to the famous Père la Chaise near Paris.[3]

Young Albert, who was indeed a child of Nature, and in sympathy with her in many of her moods, had grown tired of

---

*Probably mistletoe or, although not technically a parasite, Spanish moss.

reading the tributes of love and friendship which covered the splendid marble columns on every hand, and had taken his stand on a prominent rock which hangs out some distance over the water, and bears the name of "Lover's Leap." There are many such scattered along the streams of the South, wherever the Red man made his home, and like all others this has its legend. It was there, according to tradition, a young warrior and a beautiful daughter of his chief and tribe, whose consent they could not gain for their marriage, held their last affectionate conference, and with locked hands threw themselves from the jutting rock into the rushing torrent and sent their souls united to the Spirit land.

Albert was deeply engaged in thinking of the legend, and the fate of the aboriginees who had been so cruelly driven from their homes and hunting grounds by the superior force and oftimes cruel power of the Anglo-Saxon race[4], when he turned his gaze to the splendid picture of Nature and art combined, which renders this "silent city of the dead" so famous, and beheld a young female seated upon a small mound in the rear of where he stood. Judging from her earnest gaze and flushed features, she was evidently viewing the surrounding scenery with an appreciative eye, and fully alive to its every aspect of romantic beauty.

II

The Return to Camp

THE SIGHT of the beautiful creature that crossed Albert's gaze led our hero to believe that she was not really a human being, but a wood nymph or fairy who had made this beautiful and lovely spot her abiding place, and was the presiding genius of the scene. Not until he had approached so near as to disturb her reveries and attract her glance, and had exchanged a "good evening," was this poetical illusion dispelled. At this time, the "gray uniform" was all that was necessary to introduce the Confederate soldier into Southern Society, hence Albert felt excusable for entering into conversation with the young lady. He soon ascertained she was a resident of the city, her home being near the camp of the soldiers, and Albert asked permission to accompany her to her house.[5]

In strolling through the cemetery Albert had ample opportunity to scan the features of his companion, and found her to be one of the most beautiful girls of her age he had ever met. She was of that style of beauty known as brunette, which seems to attain its highest degree of perfection beneath the sunny skies of Italy and in our own beloved sunny South. Her soft mass of black hair was unrestrained by braid or comb, and hung far down her shoulders, the sport of the gentle evening breeze; she wore a wide, tastily trimmed hat called a "sundown," which sat jauntily upon her head, beneath which flashed her large dark eyes. Her rich brunette complexion seemed to change with every sentiment she uttered, and Albert was of that tender and susceptible age, when he would have contended she did not possess a single defect, and that she was his beau ideal of female loveliness.

Albert was gratified to learn that Miss Florence was the daughter of Mrs. ———, one of the most devoted friends of the South, and more particularly of every soldier who came in contact with her. Indeed there was not a company or scarcely a mess* in Albert's command, who had not been the recipent of many substantial favors at her hands, in the shape of lunches and many little luxuries which cheer the soldier's life in camp.

Albert and Florence approached the gate to her splendid home, and he lingered as long as politeness would permit, inwardly regretting the lack of courage to tell her she had made a deep impression upon his heart. He expressed the hope that he would meet her again at Lover's Leap. To this she replied with a sweet smile; whereupon Albert bade her good evening and started for camp, his mind filled with a train of strange but happy emotions. He had not gone far, however, when he heard some one calling after him. Turning to see who it was, Albert beheld a servant who, in coming up to him said, "Sir, here is some coffee my Mistress wishes you to carry to camp and share with your comrades." Albert sent his profound thanks to Mrs. ———, and told the servant he would return the vessel the next day. The coffee proved a welcome gift, and Albert and his messmates were enabled to

---

*A small congenial group of men into which companies were informally divided to secure and prepare their own meals together (Wiley).

make a splendid supper from the contents of a box of nice things, which one of their number had received from home a few days previous.[6]

Supper being over, Albert retired for the night, and in his dreams he held Florence by the hand and pleaded for her love. But his sweet dreams, like all earthly bliss, were of short duration. His slumbers were brought to a close at early dawn by the sound of the fife and drum for "roll call."

Albert's thoughts were upon the charming young female who had such a power to conquer at a glance, and he determined to call on her that day. For that purpose, as soon as he was free, he donned his beautiful suit of gray in order to appear before her in a most captivating style.

Albert called at the residence of Mrs. ——— and stepping upon the verandah rang the bell, and was met by the servant who took the vessel in which Albert had carried the coffee to camp the day before. He handed the servant his card and was conducted into the parlor, where Florence was in readiness to receive him. She gave him such a cordial greeting that it soon made him feel at home.

By Albert's request Florence was soon seated at the piano playing "Dixie" and other Southern airs, which at that time never failed to fire the rebel heart with patriotic zeal.[7]

When Florence had finished playing, Albert led her to the divan and listened to her sprightly and graphic narration of the incidents of the previous day, and laughed heartily of their introduction at "Lover's Leap."

Florence expressed her regret at not being permitted to show him all the attractive features of the cemetery, which afforded Albert an excuse to request the pleasure of her company for another stroll to Rose Hill, which she granted, adding that nothing would give her more pleasure than to point out to him all the features of beauty connected with that romantic spot. After appointing the next day at 4 o'clock p. m. for another visit, Albert took his leave and wended his way to camp, resolving in his own mind to employ every honorable means to win the love of this sweet girl, who had made such a deep impression on his heart. This resolution was formed in ignorance of what he found afterwards to be true, that he had already inspired in Florence's bosom sentiments as tender as those he entertained for her.

Next day as the time for Albert's visit drew near, Florence stood beside a window looking toward the encampment of the soldiers. The faint sounds of music were wafted to her hearing by the gentle zephyrs; she left the window and walked out upon the verandah of her lovely residence, and beheld a beautiful sight approaching. It was a full band of musicians in gorgeous uniforms, playing one of the soul stirring airs of the period, followed by Albert's battalion in their splendid suits of gray, with their arms and accoutrements shining like burnished silver in the clear sunlight.

The officers evidently intended to make a display of the excellent condition of the command and their efficiency in the drill, and instead of going on to camp, they marched and counter marched the battalion up and down various streets, halting occasionally to rest and go through the manual of arms, and some of the most intricate and difficult movements—such as forming the hollow square, etc.—as laid down in *Gilham's Manual* for handling a regiment.

When the marchers neared the home of Florence, Albert looked eagerly for the object of his love, and beheld her on the sidewalk beautifully attired, with a large and handsome bouquet in her hand, watching closely the passing column. As Albert drew opposite to where she stood, she gave him a sweet smile of recognition and threw the flowers at his feet. He hastily and eagerly seized the precious token of her remembrance, raised his hat in acknowledgment, and was soon out of sight—the happiest youth, perhaps, in the large crowd of young and ardent soldiers.

As soon as the camp was reached and the parade dismissed, Albert made a hurried toilet, and hastened to fulfill his engagement. He found Florence on the verandah, with gloves, hat and parasol, and they at once commenced their lengthy walk.

III

To the Front

IT WOULD BE SUPERFLUOUS to detail all that occurred between Albert and Florence in the course of that warm afternoon walk. It was September, and no difference could be seen in the landscape or gardens. If some of the more fragrant exotics of spring had ceased to bloom, they were replaced by the more brilliant but odorless flowers of autumn.

The grove around Rose Hill looked as green, and the scene within its sacred precincts as bright as in the early spring, and the air was a perfect tangle of bird songs, chirps and cooings, resting now and then upon the monotone of the limpid brook that rushes along through the cemetery, soon to be lost in the remorseless river.

Albert and Florence were young and susceptible, and as the spark of mutual love was already burning in their bosoms, it is not at all strange that it was fanned into flame by the enchanting influence of the scene.

These walks were repeated almost daily, and this innocent but imprudent couple became inseparable. They had no past, there was no thought of the future; there was only the intoxicating present—it was first love: that soul stirring passion every ardent bosom has felt, that sentiment that makes one feel and know what the Garden was before the serpent entered, that passion which time cannot efface, the recollection that the trials and triumphs of life cannot dim, but ever remains with us an inspiration and a hope.

Three weeks went by so quickly that our young friends would have believed they had scarcely been a day in each other's society. Every moment Albert could spare from his duties was spent with Florence, in daily walks to the cemetery or in sweet converse at her home interspersed with music; for Florence was one of the best singers and performers in Macon, a city that has always been celebrated for its cultivation of this divine science, and the fine amateur talent of its vocalists and pianists of both sexes.

Albert and Florence were happy and perfectly oblivious of everything but their own mutual love. They had ceased to remember that a great revolution was in progress, stirring this great country from centre to circumference. The immense armies of the North were on their way to the South, and the soil of Georgia had already resounded to the tramp of the enemy's legions. The mountains of her northern border were even then echoing along their valleys the harsh and alien sounds of hostile shot and shell—valleys that had known nothing but peace since the war whoop of the savage, as he gazed for the last time upon his pursuers, and defiantly turned his face to the setting sun in obedience to the decree of destiny.

Such history was far from the minds of the young pair, however. Yet, while they were seated on one of the rustic seats that are tastily scattered through the cemetery, exchanging tender sentiments of regard, they were startled by the loud, rapid sounds of the drum as it sent the sharp echos of the long roll away to the hills for miles around. Albert sprang to his feet like a startled deer, and Florence, becoming terrified by the sudden emotion that had seized upon her young lover, desired to know the cause of his great excitement. His only answer was to say to her that they must at once return to the city, as it was necessary for him to reach camp as soon as possible.

Leaving Florence at the gate of her residence, Albert hurried to camp, and learned from his comrades, who had been left to look after the camp equipage, that the battalion had received orders to proceed to the front, and had gone to the depot to take the cars. Albert buckled on his cartridge box, shouldered his gun, bade his remaining comrades a hasty farewell and went to join his regiment at the railroad. Of course he called to say good bye to Florence.

This proved to be the most trying ordeal our young hero was ever called upon to pass through. He possessed a brave soul, and felt that he would not falter before the enemies of his country, but when he found Florence in tears, and as he strained her to his heart and imprinted upon her lips a long burning kiss of mingled love and sorrow, he felt his resolution falter, and he hastened away, fearing the influence such emotions would have upon him. Many such scenes were gone through during that long bloody war, and nearly every young soldier had his experience of this sort to relate. Many young hearts were torn asunder by the stern call of duty, never to be reunited this side of the grave.

Albert also took leave of Florence's kind mother, who said she would pray for his safety, and begged of him to visit them again as soon as possible.

On his way to the depot, Albert had to traverse some of the principal streets of the city, and soon perceived, by the large crowds of excited, anxious looking citizens, and the loaded drays, and several batteries of artillery going to the railroad, that there had been some terrible news received from General Bragg's army.

Upon inquiring of an obliging officer, he learned that the Federal army had left its entrenchments around Chattanooga, marched into Georgia, and were met by the Confederate troops on the banks of Chickamauga creek where a terrible battle was then going on between the two armies. The officer also informed him that orders had been received to hurry reinforcements to the front, and to provide hospital accommodation for a large number of wounded. This information led Albert to conclude that Georgia, so long exempt, would now be called upon to experience some of those horrors of war to which the people of Virginia and other border states had been forced to submit. This opinion was more than confirmed before his regiment reached Atlanta, as they passed several long trains of cars filled with the blue uniformed Soldiers of the Union who had been made prisoners by the boys in gray.

They also met numbers of wounded rebels, who were suffering from every character of wound that could possibly be inflicted by the terrible engines of destruction which the devilish ingenuity of their enemy could inspire. Yet they were cheerful and uncomplaining, and seemed to be much more interested in the issue of the battle than their own sufferings.

The contrast between them and the Federal prisoners was very marked. Many of the latter were foreigners of the lowest type, unable to speak a word of English, who had been hired for a paltry sum to do the fighting of men who remained at home to grow rich upon Government contracts. Those who possessed any intelligence were very reticent, and appeared as though they had little sympathy with the policy of making war upon helpless women and children. Indeed they looked haggard and mean, as men who are detected in a disreputable act.

The Confederate wounded, many of whom Albert talked

with, informed him that General Bragg had been reinforced by the splendid *corps d'armee* of General Longstreet, of the army of Northern Virginia, that the troops were in good spirits, and no doubt the issue of the engagement would be a grand victory for our Southern cause.

IV

Old Quarters

ALBERT HAD LITTLE TIME to think of Florence *en route* to Atlanta, as his mind was absorbed with thoughts of war, and everything he saw and heard kept that subject uppermost in his mind.

Arriving in the city he found the car-shed,* the streets, and hotels filled with wounded officers and men, and couriers rushing madly around, all of whom seemed much excited. Large crowds of noncombatants, and that egotistical class of "street corner Generals," of which every military post in the South had a large number during the war, were discussing the fate of the battle, and their fears were so excited that many were making hasty preparations to take their families away from the city, fully believing the Yankees were thundering at the very gates of the city, instead of being on the border of the State, one hundred miles away.

The battalion made temporary headquarters in a large building, and as the great battle of Chickamauga had been fought and won by the Confederates, our young and ardent

*The old Atlanta Depot, or Passenger House, built in 1854 near the present site of Zero Mile Post in Underground Atlanta; destroyed by Sherman ten years later.

little battalion expressed many regrets at being too late to aid in driving the invaders from the sacred soil of Georgia. Instead, they were detailed to perform the very important, but distasteful duties of the Provost Marshal's department.

They spent several days amid the scenes to be witnessed always in the rear of large armies after an important battle, heartily tired of seeing frightened women, and were disgusted with the great number of strong, able-bodied men who spent their time in criticising the conduct of our Generals, instead of going boldly to the front to aid in driving back the enemies of our country. It was good news to the boys when the order came for the battalion to return to their old quarters at Macon. The return trip was without incident. The pleasure our young friends anticipated in taking up their quarters again in the Central City would have been greatly enhanced if they had been allowed to participate in the great battle.[8]

The battalion was marched through the streets and attracted the eager gaze of thousands. The windows of every mansion were filled with ladies, who manifested their pleasure by smiles and waving of handkerchiefs.

Albert had written Florence that the battle had ended before his command reached Atlanta, and that it was probable that he would return very soon to renew his pledges of life-long devotion.

When he had finished his duties at camp, he hurried off to see Florence, his heart aglow with all those tender emotions which can only be inspired by first love.

Florence's reception proved to Albert that her love had not grown cold, and he felt that she would always remain as true to him as the needle to the pole, or the stream to the sea. Yet her pale cheek and anxious expression led him to believe something unusual had occurred to give her trouble, and he pressed her to tell him the cause of her unhappiness. She informed him that Captain Winston, an officer who was acting as military conductor on one of the railroads leading from the city, had been visiting her for some months. She had regarded him as a pleasant social acquaintance, and had never regarded him in any other light than that of a friend, until he had startled her upon a recent visit by a violent declaration of love.

Florence told Albert that she was no less astonished than grieved at Captain Winston's declaration, and that after thanking the Captain for the compliment he paid her in offering her his devotion, assured him it was impossible to reciprocate it, as her heart had already been given to another.

This seemed to make Captain Winston furious, and he left her presence in such a state of mind that she feared a meeting between Albert and the Captain would culminate in bloodshed, as the latter had intimated that he knew the man who had dared to enter the lists against him as a rival for Florence's heart and hand.

Florence begged Albert to avoid Captain Winston's society as much as possible, and not allow himself provoked into a difficulty, which would grieve her beyound expression, as it might force her mother to forbid further association with Albert.

After promising to obey Florence's request, and pledging his word of honor to do nothing hasty or precipitate, Albert took his leave and returned to camp to reflect upon the proper plan to pursue, fully realizing for the first time in his life that the course of true love never runs smoothly.

Albert was very young and ignorant of the ways of the world. He had never had a difficulty with any one, and had never thought that it would be necessary for him to become a party to a personal quarrel, as he did not entertain ill will against any human being.

Such was his faith in Florence that Captain Winston's

admiration for her had not roused in Albert the bitter feeling of jealousy, and he could not account for the Captain's intention to persecute her with his attention, as he did not see how a gentleman could continue to love a woman who had refused to reciprocate his affection.

When Albert thought of the difference in age, rank and position between himself and Captain Winston, he fully appreciated the advantage his rival would have over him in the conduct of a jealous love affair.

V

The Rival Met

THE DAINTY little notes accompanying Florence's daily presents of bouquets and sandwiches were promptly replied to by Albert, in which he took occasion to express his sentiments freely in regard to Captain Winston's heartless conduct in using his superiority of rank and power to crush a rival who had no means to counteract such conduct, so unbecoming an officer and a gentleman.

Albert had never been introduced to his rival, but knew him well by sight, and the Captain also knew Albert. Whenever they passed each other on the street, Captain Winston made known his feelings toward Albert by a savage glare and contemptuous toss of his head, which were so significant and full of hatred that Albert knew this would lead to something serious should circumstances arise that would make it necessary for them to meet. This could not be long avoided, as batches of prisoners were almost daily arriving in the city, from the front, *en route* for Andersonville, and a guard was always detailed from the battalion to escort them to that now famous place of confinement for the enemies of our country.

Captain Winston was military conductor on the railroad

that led from Macon to Andersonville, and should Albert be detailed as a guard, he knew his only chance to avoid a meeting with his rival rested upon the mere chance of leaving the city when Captain Winston should be at the other end of the line, as it required two officers to act as military conductors on the railroad.

Albert had imparted his fears to Florence, and she, like a true girl, told him to avoid any cause of a difficulty, but if the issue was forced upon him, to meet it courageously, assuring him she would never cease to love him until he proved himself unworthy of her confidence.

Thus assured, our young hero determined to act entirely upon the defensive, and to defend his honor, if attacked, even at the sacrifice of his life.

He did not have long to wait for an opportunity to meet his rival. On the afternoon of the day of his last visit to Florence, a detail of a sergeant and six men was required of his battalion to escort to Andersonville a small party of prisoners that had been captured in a skirmish between the two hostile armies, which were still confronting each other on the line of Tennessee and Georgia.

Albert's name was included in the detail, and early next morning Sergeant Rawson formed his detachment, marched to the prison camp, took charge of the prisoners, proceeded to the depot and got aboard the cars, which were already standing under the car-shed awaiting the time of departure.

As soon as they had secured seats for the prisoners, Albert perceived Captain Winston walking up and down the depot floor, and while it was not uncommon for soldiers to go armed, yet he could not account for the cause of Captain Winston's wearing a brace of Navy revolvers while he was not on duty at the front, unless it was to impress upon the passengers who happened not to possess the right sort of papers, that he was a very dangerous character.

The solution of the Captain's haughty and imperious bearing was not long delayed. The hands of the clock which regulated the running of the schedules of the railroads marked the hour of the train's departure; the voice of the conductor was heard to ring out in no uncertain tones: "All aboard!" which acted like magic upon the passengers who intended leaving, summoning them instantly to rush for their seats; the whistle sounded, and the train was moving off for its long run to Andersonville.

The countenances of the prisoners indicated that they fully realized the fact that they would be confined in that horrible stockade of Andersonville. Full and graphic descriptions of the horrors of that prison had been furnished by soldiers of the Federal armies who had undergone, for a season, its loathsome tortures, and the Northern papers teemed with these stories, which were used to stimulate hatred of the South and to encourage volunteering to put down the rebellion.

Such was the terror that had been inspired by a recital of the horrors of Andersonville, that prisoners were bold to affirm, in language that carried conviction with it, that they preferred death to confinement within the walls of that stockade of sixteen acres of ground, where more than thirty thousand of their comrades were sweltering beneath the rays of a semi-tropical sun without sufficient food, water, or any comfort to mitigate prison life, which is to be dreaded under any circumstances.

Such thoughts as these filled the mind of our hero, and now, when more than a decade has passed since the immortal Lee gave up his sword, and the battle-scarred remnant of his army laid down their arms in defeat, but without dishonor—now, when our hero reverts to this incident in his early experience as a soldier, he is able to account for that bloody struggle between the sections, and he has learned also that

Andersonville and its horrors will ever remain a dark and ineffaceable stain upon the civilization of the nineteenth century, has been the impediment to a speedy return to civil government, and the cause of the long reign of terror in the South since peace was declared. It has been equaled in its prostrating effects upon the country only by the war and war's attending Evils.[9]

Albert was sympathizing so deeply with the prisoners that he had almost forgotten his own position, when Captain Winston entered the car at the opposite end from which he was sitting, to discharge his duties as military conductor.

After he had scrutinized the papers of the soldiers in the car, he approached the seat Albert was occupying and commenced a conversation with him in a very offensive and insulting manner:

"I suppose, sir, you are Miss Florence's tutor, and have instructed her whom to receive visits and attention from, and whom to avoid."

"Not disputing your word," replied Albert, "I do no such thing; but I advise her as to what I think is best, and leave her to judge for herself who among her acquaintances are worthy of her friendship and who are not."

"You think it would be best for her to discard you or I one, do you?"

"I do," replied Albert.

"And you think she will decide in your favor, of course, do you not?"

"I have not said so," answered Albert.

"But you have peremptorily demanded that she make a decision in favor of one or the other of us?"

"I have, sir, but how did you get in possession of this knowledge, Captain Winston?"

The Captain winced under this question as though he had resorted to some dishonorable means to acquire the information, but Albert did not intend that he should evade a direct and unequivocal answer to his question. Instead of replying to the question, the Captain, who gave unmistakable signs of anger, put his hand upon one of the pistols he so conspicuously displayed, as if he meant to frighten our hero, but the movement failed to have the desired effect.

Albert rose to his feet as soon as he suspected the Captain's intention to draw his weapon, and asked in a very decided tone:

"Captain Winston, I demand of you, upon the honor of a gentleman, to inform me how you have become informed of my advice to Miss Florence?"

"Perhaps it would be prudent in me not to answer your question. It might induce you to take the precaution to seal your *billet-doux* hereafter."

The idea that Captain Winston would use such disreputable means to get the advantage of him, thereby disgracing the uniform he wore, and forfeiting every claim to recognition as a gentleman, created such indignation in Albert's bosom he could control himself no longer, but replied with flashing eye and quivering frame:

"Captain Winston, you are a low-flung scoundrel, and nothing but the difference in rank between us prevents me from pinning you to the wall of this car with my bayonet!"

VI

The Challenge

CAPTAIN WINSTON'S only reply to Albert's language was to draw from the belt around his waist one of the pistols he carried and level it at Albert's head; but before he could fire his weapon, Albert raised his musket and brought it to a "charge" against the Captain's breast, with the intention of plunging it into his heart. He was prevented from doing so only by Captain Winston himself, who lowered his pistol and seized Albert's bayonet to save his own life, and by a desperate effort, succeeded in wrenching it from the barrel of the gun.

While this struggle was going on, Albert cocked his gun to fire, and was in the act of discharging his musket, when the cap was knocked from the tube by one of the guards.

The young soldier who had thus saved Captain Winston's life was a powerful man physically, and with the grasp of a giant, he disarmed the Captain.

During this struggle between the guard and Winston, Albert seized the gun which the soldier had left at his seat when he interposed to prevent a fight, and was watching for an opportunity to carry out his determination to shoot his antagonist, as he was thoroughly aroused and thirsted for vengeance.

The excitement in the car was very great, and if the prisoners had made an effort, they could have easily escaped, as they were entirely forgotten in the struggle between the two rebels.

The guards had surrounded and got between the combatants, and one of them, a particular friend and messmate of Albert's made a strong appeal to Albert by telling him his adversary had been disarmed, and asking him if he would seek to injure an unarmed foe.

The influence of this friend had the desired effect upon Albert, who promised to let the matter drop for the present, and as Captain Winston had been pushed out on the platform and taken refuge in another car, peace and quiet was restored.[10]

This incident was of so much importance that the sergeant and all of his guards ceased to think of the terrible fate that awaited their prisoners, and they were so engaged in discussing the causes and inevitable issue of the struggle between their comrade and the valiant Captain, that they lost all interest in the trip, and were only roused to a recollection of the purpose of their mission by the loud tones of the brakeman of the train, who shouted at the top of his voice, "Andersonville!"

The effect of this announcement upon the prisoners was very marked—they turned deadly pale, and trembled in every limb.

There was quite a crowd collected at the depot, as usual, but with the arrival of prisoners occurring almost daily, this last addition to the thousands who were already in "durance vile"* at that famous and infamous pen, excited little notice or comment.

Some of the soldiers belonging to the garrison were

*Wretched imprisonment (poetic).

present, and indulged in such remarks as, "Hello, more Yanks!"—"Take 'em over to the bull-pen, boys, plenty of room—all front rooms not taken yet—bedrooms with parlors attached still to let at Jeff Davis' hotel," and other remarks uttered in that spirit to make light of every subject, grave or gay, which was true of the soldiers of both armies during the war.

Albert and his companions were shocked at this language, but learned before leaving the place, from conversations held with numbers of the garrison, that they had seen enough of human suffering and prison life, and longed to be transferred to active duty in the field, infinitely preferring to risk the chance of battle to being forced to gaze continually upon the sickening and heart rending scenes of human suffering.

Albert and his comrades shared these sentiments, and said if there was anything calculated to dampen their patriotism and cause them to lose all interest in their country's struggle for independence, it would be an order sending them to that place to guard prisoners.

This being the state of their feelings, they felt greatly relieved after they had delivered the prisoners and learned they were to return to Macon on the next train, which came thundering along in about four hours, and our hero and his comrades gazed upon Andersonville for the last time. And here we will let the curtain fall upon this place which has been a fruitful source of much hatred and bitterness towards the South after the war.

The ride to Macon was devoid of anything exciting, but was very much enjoyed by all the guards except Albert, who knew that he had incurred the hatred of a man who had plainly shown, by intercepting his letters to the woman both were anxious to win, that he was capable of resorting to any means to overcome an adversary and rid himself of what he firmly believed was the only obstacle to Florence's heart and hand.

About ten o'clock the next morning a very handsome young officer in a new uniform with the bars of first Lieutenant, came up to Albert's quarters and introduced himself *a la militaire*, as Lieutenant Marcus, a friend of Captain Winston's, handing Albert at the same time the following letter:

MACON, GA. Feb. ——, 1864

MR. ALBERT—SIR:—After your disgraceful conduct on board the cars yesterday, I am forced to demand that you meet me outside the limits of the State, and render me satisfaction for the public insult you have placed upon me, according to those terms which are contained in the Code for adjusting difficulties between gentlemen. This is a time when civil law is subservient to the military, and should it be impossible for you to obtain permission to leave the State, and believing you would prefer to be buried on the soil of Georgia—name any place near the city for a meeting to-morrow morning at eight o'clock, and I will give you a passport to hell without charge. This will be handed to you by my friend, Lieutenant Fred. Marcus.

I remain Respectfully,
JOHN A. WINSTON
Captain, C. S. A.

VII

The Reply

THE SURVIVORS of the war—on both sides—for whose benefit this record of personal experiences is mainly written, will appreciate the isolated and helpless condition of Albert. The relation existing between a private soldier and a commissioned officer was as great as the imagination could grasp.

Here was a youth, reared on a farm in one of the most remote regions of his native State, who had been induced to join the army under an excitement mistaken for patriotism at a time when he should have been at home under the care and protection of his parents, and who had innocently incurred the hatred of a man who bore the rank of Captain. This man had compromised his position by engaging in a low and disreputable fight with a private soldier who was his inferior in rank and position and who had no friend who could possibly aid him, as his comrades were like himself, either privates or noncommissioned officers. Albert knew full well if he had accepted the terms laid down in his enemy's note he would have been mobbed, or arrested and court martialed, hence he determined to put in execution the plan agreed upon with Florence, as the only means by which he had any hope of circumventing his unscrupulous rival.

Acting upon this resolution, he drew up the following reply to Captain Winston's coarse, insulting and defiant note:

CAMP NEAR MACON, GA.
Feb. ——, 1864.

CAPTAIN WINSTON—SIR:—Your note by the hand of Lt. Marcus is received. My ignorance of the code of honor, the absence of a friend through whom I ought to send this reply to you, and the difference of rank and age existing between us, which is a barrier to such a meeting as you propose, must be my excuse for sending this reply through the post. While I confess to you my ignorance of the code, yet I have always heard that the challenged party has the right to choose weapons, but I am willing to waive this right, if you will agree to the following proposition:

You are aware, sir, that our lives belong to our bleeding country, and we have no right to sacrifice them in a personal conflict, until our land is free and peace reestablished. We will, each of us, go to the regular army and join some command in active service, and do battle side by side. I suggest the Sixteenth battalion of Cavalry, now under Gen. John Morgan. If we shall be so fortunate as to survive the dangers incident to war we will, when peace is declared, select each a comrade and settle this difficulty with the weapons we used in our country's defense. If this proposition meets your approbation, please meet me at the Provost Marshal's office to-morrow morning, to be mustered into service.

Hoping that the scenes and struggles that we may encounter on the battle field will satiate your thirst for blood, and cause you to withdraw your challenge, I subscribe myself your obedient servant,

ALBERT

P.S. Should you fail to accept my proposition, I will publish your correspondence, and show you up as being so cowardly that you refuse to face the enemies of our country on the field of battle.

ALBERT

After sending the reply to the challenge, Albert wrote to Florence as follows:

MY DEAR FLORENCE:—It is with reluctance that I inform you I will leave the city to-morrow morning to join the regular army, where I will remain until the war is ended, unless I am killed in defense of home, loved ones and liberty. May the God of mercy guide, guard and protect you until I return to take you to my bosom—to love and protect you till death do us part.

Let me assure you, my dearest one, that I do not blame you for anything that has taken place. All I regret is that I have brought trouble upon you, and caused the sunshine of your genial nature to become clouded with vexation—to be able to decorate your pathway with flowers is the most ardent desire of your devoted lover,

ALBERT

Captain Winston met Albert at the office of the Provost Marshal on the following day, according to request, and they were both mustered into service, and received promise of transportation to any part of the army they might desire to go to.

Captain Winston, after a few days spent in making preparation, left Macon to join the command under General Morgan.

Soon after Albert left camp, it was reported that he had gone to meet Captain Winston for the purpose of fighting a duel. A Lieutenant with a squad of men was sent to arrest him. They marched to the city and met Albert on Cherry street, and placed him under arrest. Albert demanded their authority, to which the Lieutenant replied: "I have orders from headquarters to arrest you, and carry you to camp."

Albert replied that he had been transferred to the regular army, and producing his papers from the Provost Marshal, was immediately released.

He then returned to camp to make preparation for immediate departure for the front, for the purpose of uniting with the Cavalry branch of service, hoping to do his country good service, and at the same time prove to Captain Winston that he was worthy of the love that Florence had bestowed upon him.

Albert spent a few days with his friends and relatives in Butts county before his final departure to the front, and while at home, learned that the command of General Morgan had gone on a raid into the enemy's country, which would make it very hazardous for recruits to join him.

After being informed of the situation in Tennessee, Albert determined to join the army of Northern Virginia, where he had an older brother in the service. Having made the necessary preparation, our hero lost no time in making his final departure.

Albert did not regret the fact that he would have to pass through Macon; nor did he make any complaint when he was informed that he would be compelled to wait five hours in Macon, in order to meet the train bound for Augusta. He took advantage of this delay, and called on Florence for the purpose of bidding her an affectionate farewell.

It was a cold dreary day, and the shades of evening were gathering in the lonely depths of the forest, and Albert and Florence were walking silently through the long avenues which the lofty trees made with their stately columns.

It was only when the swift falling shadows betokened the near approach of night, that Florence turned in the direction of her beautiful residence and said, "We must return; it is getting very late."

"Thank you," replied Albert, curtly. "You have called the fact to my mind, that I am to take the train at six o'clock, and before that time I must bid you a long farewell."

The bitter words stung her heart. Tears sprang to her eyes, and her voice trembled as she said:

"Albert do you, can you, believe that I want to end this last interview? God knows, and you know yourself that I would prolong these hours eternally if it were in my power."

VIII

The Parting Interview

To walk and talk together,
Filled their cup of joy;
For she was a rich young lady,
And loved her soldier boy.

THE PARTING SCENES may appear superfluous to the reader, except those like Albert and Florence, who had pledged to each other a life-long devotion, and pictured for themselves a bright future, but had all their joyous hopes crushed by the cruel hand of war.

With the close of this chapter, we will drop the curtain over the affectionate scenes of Albert and Florence, and follow the Rivals through the exciting scenes of war till they met and settled the difficulty between them.

The twilight had cast its dusky vail over the forest in which Albert and Florence were walking, and the shadows were momentarily deepened with the approach of night.

As they neared the home of Florence, he held her by the hand, and in an agitated tone of voice, said:

"Florence, it is very doubtful whether we will ever meet again. When we part I will cross the line of the State before the sun rises to-morrow morning, and I will never return until liberty is perched upon our banner, or our beloved cause crushed by the superior force of the invader. And should I be so fortunate as to survive the perils of war, I will then have to perform the unpleasant task of killing your former friend, or lose my own life in vindication of my honor."

"Promise me," she said, with a tender quiver of pain in her voice, "that you will have no difficulty with Captain Winston if there is any way consistent to avoid it."

"I have never sought a difficulty with him," replied Albert, "and I shall certainly try to avoid it in the future as far as consistent with true manliness; but unless he retracts, he or I one will never return to Georgia."

She drew her hand from his and covered her face; for a moment she struggled for composure; sobs burst from her, and tears rained fast through her locked fingers.

"Let me, before we part, be assured that you will not quite forget me," she wept, "that you will think of me often—not sadly, nor regretfully, but tenderly, as one who would share your success, or with the same cheerfulness share your sorrows and misfortures."

"I will think of you always," he whispered; "You will be the guiding star—the inspiration of my life; no matter what may be my fate, I will hold you nearest my heart through all the struggles I encounter, and the hope of meeting you again after the struggle is over, will be my thoughts' incentive to win the victory for our country, and encircle my brow with laurels. I will have but one object in view, and that will be to return to you worthy of the prize that awaits me."

The wind had sunk into a whisper, and a cold desolate silence brooded over all things.

When they reached the home of Florence, the time for parting had arrived. Albert held her by the hand, and pulling her toward him, kissed her tenderly as he bid her farewell, and he was gone.

She looked after him until the black depths of twilight hid his form, and then turned to retire to her room, where she could relieve her aching heart by giving vent to a flood of tears.

IX

On to Richmond

THE NIGHT WAS coming down gloomily with threatening tokens of rain, the clouds gathering across the pale blue sky; all combined to depress Albert in mind, and cause him to shudder at the thought of coming events. But his thoughts could not dwell on the dark side of the picture. The moving of the cars as they sped out of the quiet city across the Ocmulgee and through the pine forest in the direction of Augusta, soon diverted Albert's thoughts from the parting scenes, and dropping his head on the back of his seat, he was soon in the arms of Morpheus. He knew of little that passed until he reached Augusta.

By the time that the first bright line of crimson light had made its appearance in the east, preceeded by the mild twinkle of the morning star, he had secured a seat on another train that was to carry him further on towards his destination.

When the train began to move off, Albert thought of having told Florence that he would cross the line of the State before sunrise, and he stepped out on the platform of the car and beheld the surrounding scenery with an appreciative eye, fully alive to every feature of magnificence and grandeur.

Beneath the train were the rippling waters of the Savannah river, moving on in silent majesty. On the one bank could be seen the grand old Empire State, and on the other was the proud Palmetto State, each claiming its share of stately grandeur.

As the train emerged from the bridge, Albert took one last lingering look across the river, as if he could not bear the thought of taking the last view of Georgia, his Mother State. All his childhood scenes and joys rushed into his thoughts with such force that his manhood was completely overcome, and he gave way to the weaker emotions of his nature, and wept like a child. But he would not dwell upon sad reflections; his mind was soon diverted from those thoughts by the new scenery that greeted him on every side. The stately mansions by the roadside, with their beautiful flower gardens—the pride of the fair ones of the Palmetto State—were among the features of interest that attracted attention, contrasted with the swamps and lagoons that are so conspicuous along the route to Wilmington, North Carolina. At this place our hero spent one night very pleasantly, and on the following morning after taking a stroll through the city, he mounted the iron horse and was soon speeding on through the pine forest to Goldsboro, thence to Weldon and Petersburg. On the subsequent morning, before the sun had made its appearance, Albert got a glimpse of the lofty spires of the far famed city of Richmond.

Albert, after his arrival, spent one day in the ill-fated city, where he saw many things of interest to him. Here it was that he met his former captain, who commanded the company to which Albert had belonged, and who had gone to Richmond to see President Davis in regard to having the battalion permanently detailed at Andersonville to guard prisoners. Captain M. did not know that Albert had left his company to enlist in Virginia, and his astonishment can well be imagined when he met him in the street at the Confederate Capital. He told Albert of the arrangments that had been made with the President to help the battalion in the local service during the war, and begged Albert to return with him to Georgia, promising to keep him out of the war; but Albert thanked him for his kindness, telling him that he could not be satisfied in the local service while his country was bleeding at every pore. The captain wished him well, and with a few words of advice, parted to meet no more.

Albert visited all the places of attraction during the day; he went into the halls of the Confederate Congress and listened to the stormy debate on the conscript question, and other issues of the day.[11]

On the following day he took passage on the train running toward Gordonsville, which soon brought him in sight of the Blue Ridge Mountains, around the base of which the A. N. V. was camped.

The picturesque scenery of the mountains, and the grand display of infantry and cavalry all combined to kindle a flame of patriotism in Albert's breast, and made him feel perfectly at home when he was greeted by the soldiers in camp.

The duties that were performed at this point were but a pleasant pastime, doing picket duty and scouting along the little Rapidan river and around the base of the mountains, interspersed with an occasional drill or dress parade, or general review of the army. This was all that was required of the soldiers while in winter quarters; but the approach of the spring campaign threw a damper over the feelings of many of the old veterans, who knew by experience what it would bring forth.[12]

On the morning of the 4th of May, they heard the distant war thunder away to the east. Orders were received to prepare four days' rations, and be ready to move at a moment's warning. The camp was all astir, preparing for the march; but before they had time to prepare rations, the command, "Fall in! Fall in!" was heard throughout the camp.

X

Chancellorsville

IN A FEW MOMENTS a long line of bayonets and muskets was glittering along the turnpike, as the troops moved on toward the Rapidan, along whose banks the roar of cannon and the rattle of musketry were heard, vying with each other amid the strife and carnage of battle. Lee and his adversary were contesting the field; the historic battle in the wilderness of Chancellorsville was being fought. The troops moved on steadily in the direction of the conflict, believing that the Federals had only made a demonstration on the right, or had sent out a reconnoitering party that would be very easily repulsed.

The troops had a great deal of fun and jest in regard to the result, and as they marched along, the old decks of cards were drawn from their hiding places and strewn for miles along the road.[13]

At night on May the 4th the soldiers filed out into the woods to camp for the night.

This was Albert's first experience in getting supper without a bucket to carry water, a tray in which to make up bread, or any sign of a cooking utensil. But when he saw the other soldiers begin to peel the bark from the trees to use as a substitute for a tray in which to make bread, binding it up in paper or cloth to keep the grit from it while cooking in the ashes, he followed their example. Taking a shirt from his knapsack and tearing off one of the sleeves, he filled it with dough made in one of the bark trays, then placed it in the fire, covered it with ashes, and soon produced a delicious supper for a hungry rebel.[14]

May the 5th, at the first dawn of day, the pickets of both parties opened a brisk fire, which soon put the army in motion, ready for the clash of arms. The portion of the army to which Albert belonged was moving to and fro during the day until late in the afternoon.

When the battle began to assume a more formidable struggle than was anticipated, the soldiers learned that what they first thought to be only a faint demonstration was destined to be the most obstinate struggle of the war. Assault after assault was being made by the massed columns of the advancing Federal army, and each assault had been repulsed by the gallant corps of Ewell, until about four o'clock in the afternoon, when the superior force of the enemy began to lap their extended columns around the right wing of the Confederate column. This made it necessary for the part of the army to which Albert belonged to take their position in line of battle and extend the line of the Confederates.

It was at this point that Albert first got a view of the immortal Lee, who, on a slight eminence near where the battle was raging, had taken his position to observe the movements of the enemy. Just as the column moved up to where he stood, a halt of a few moments was ordered, which gave our hero a chance to scan the features of the General, whose fame had become world wide.

While Lee was standing in that position, a column of Yankees could be seen emerging from a dense thicket, directly in front of where the men stood, and less than two hundred yards away, moving across the corner of an old field, bearing to the right, as if trying to turn the flank of the struggling Confederate.

Just then one of the soldiers called out to General Lee, and said:

"General Lee, look at the Yankees, they will kill you if you don't get to the rear!"

To this he made no reply, nor paid any attention, but stood as firm as a statue, with his eagle eye scanning the movements of the army. By his side stood the most handsome looking officer of the army of Northern Virginia, General J. E. B. Stuart. He was dressed in a beautiful uniform, with cavalry sash, sabre and golden spurs glittering in the sun, and a long plume waving in the breeze. This gay cavalier made a considerable contrast to the unassuming Lee, with his faded suit of rebel gray.

By this time the army had been put in position for a general engagement, and with the word, "Forward, march!" the entire line moved forward, and for long hours the two powerful armies poured out their blood. Friend and foe went together down into the harvest of death.

Near dark the portion of the line where Albert was engaged was massed upon by the Federals and a desperate attempt made to break the lines. On they came, charging with steady tread amidst the tempest of death, until by the weight of numbers the Confederate line wavered and slowly receded before the torrent of Federal thousands. But after a terrible strife, the position was reestablished by nightfall, and the Confederates slept on the blood-stained field amidst the groans and prayers of the wounded and dying soldiers.

On May the 6th, the great struggle of the Wilderness was fought. At the first dawn of day the skirmisher of both armies fell back to the main line of battle, and just after light a signal was fired from a cannon on the Federal lines. The shell came crashing through the tree tops near where Albert was.

With this signal the battle opened along the entire lines. In an hour the extended lines of the Federals had lapped their left wing around the Confederate right, and thus exposed them to enfilading fire.* Longstreet's corps had not arrived on the scene of action, and the enemy having turned, the flank was rapidly approaching the rear of Hill and Ewell.

At this juncture the lines gave way, and the bullets came thick as hail from three directions. Here the Confederate loss was heavy, especially on the plank road when the enemy was near enough to demand a surrender.

Here they poured in a destructive fire, creating almost a panic. But in a few moments General Lee appeared on the scene with Longstreet's corps, that general having been wounded by an awkward shot from one of his own men. Lee determined to lead the charge in person, and would have done so, but for the remonstrance of his own men.

"To the rear!" shouted the troops as he rode to the front, "To the rear!" and a ragged Confed grasped the bit of the General's bridle, and he, whose command every soldier felt it an honor to obey, was forced to respect the command of one of his humblest subalterns.

The arrival of the immortal Lee was all that could possibly have saved the A. N. V., a part of which had become demoralized by having been flanked by the superior power of the Federal forces. The scenes at this juncture are indescribable. The turning of the flank forced the South Carolina troops from their position in line and curved them around

*Shot or missiles raked lengthwise along a line of troops.

into the part of the line held by the Georgia troops who were slightly wavering from the assaults of the brave Federals, who were pressing forward flushed with the hope of crushing the gallant Confederate before a sufficient reinforcement could arrive to check them.

The juncture of the South Carolina troops with the Georgians inspired them with confidence. The command was given for a charge, and with a terrific yell the Confederates moved forward to the most obstinate and determined conflict on record. The blood of Georgia and South Carolina ran together in pools on the ground as it streamed from the dead and dying, who fell indiscriminately on the gory field as they advanced to meet the enemy. It seemed as if no power on earth would be sufficient to stand this furious onslaught; and the flank and rear of the Confederates being unguarded, they were soon exposed to an enfilading fire so destructive it caused them to fall back.

Here our hero witnessed some deeds of heroism and daring that would have honored Caesar's legions or Bonaparte's Old Guard.

Among the braves was a young South Carolinian, scarcely sixteen years of age, who sacrificed his life in preference to turning his back to the enemy, when the Confederate lines receded. He stood like a stone wall with his breast exposed to the fire of thousands, and while shouting "Hurrah for South Carolina!" continued to fire on the enemy until a ball pierced his heart. When the fatal ball plunged into his heart, he threw up his gun, and with his hands raised above his head fell backward a corpse. Thus ended the career of as brave a boy as ever died in defense of his country. Perhaps some fond mother that was yearning to hold him again to her heart never learned the fate of her darling, who fell in the Wilderness far away from loved ones, lost from his comrades, and died while doing his duty by the side of Georgians. The immortal deeds of our Jackson, Stuart or Morgan, do not surpass the imperishable courage shown by this daring young South Carolinian, whose bones lie bleaching in the soil of Virginia.

XI

Wounded

AS THE CONFEDERATE troops fell back they were pressed on every side. They had but one way of escape. This place had been kept open by the North Carolina troops who had taken position in the rear of the Georgia troops to support them. As the Georgians and South Carolinians fell back to where their support was, they made a stand and a most desperate struggle followed, but in this, like all other struggles between them, the superior courage and gallantry of the Confederates were crushed by the superior force of numbers of the enemy. Being outnumbered more than five to one, they were forced from their position and driven back with terrible slaughter. A scene followed that beggars description. The braves of Georgia, South Carolina, North Carolina and Alabama were all massed together in the wildest excitement. Men shouting rally, officers commanding a halt, generals forgetting their danger and rushing to and fro through the confusion, couriers dashing wildly around on their excited horses, made a scene indescribable. The arrival of the gallant corps of Longstreet turned the scale and the confusion changed to the other side.

Being reinforced at last, the Confederates advanced with

Longstreet's corps. The gray lines surged forward and the Federals gave way until the ground was literally covered with dead and wounded.

Here, amidst the dense cloud of smoke, and the flash and flame of those death dealing instruments of war, Albert fell, severely wounded.

His wound, though painful and serious, was only a flesh wound, and had it not been for the loss of blood he would not have lain during the entire day and listened at the clatter of the musketry, as the contending armies wavered back and forth over the bloody field until the enemy, baffled and checked at every point, withdrew at nightfall and moved off in the direction of Spottsylvania Court House.

On the following day, the din of battle had lulled into almost perfect silence, except occasionally, away to the right, could still be heard the distant war thunder, caused by the firing of Fitzhugh Lee's light batteries at the advance of the Federal army.

While Albert lay upon the field he did not suffer much from pain, but too weak from loss of blood to leave the battle ground, he began to meditate upon what had taken place and wonder how it was that he was still alive while so may of his comrades were lying cold in death. His thoughts turned to home and loved ones, and above all the lovely form, the sweet smile and tender lovely voice of Florence, with their sweet memories, crowded into his thoughts, which reminded him of her photograph, and taking it from his bosom he stained it with kisses. And while thus passing his time he concluded to write to Florence and let her know of his condition and whereabouts. The litter corps were busily engaged in carrying the wounded from the field, taking the most critical cases first. He knew that he could send a letter through by them to the ambulance corps, thence to the railroad and on to Georgia. He took a small portfolio from his pocket, in which some letter paper and envelopes had been neatly preserved, and resting on his elbow wrote the following letter:

LYING ON THE BATTLE FIELD NEAR
CHANCELLORSVILLE, VA.
May 7th, 1864.

MY DEAR FLORENCE—I am wounded painfully, though not dangerously. The great army of Northern Virginia and army of the Potomac met yesterday in battle. The struggle was desperate and deadly. We have to mourn the loss of many gallant comrades slain. I do not believe our loss will exceed twenty thousand men, while that of the enemy is more than double that number; they having so many more engaged and their columns massed, our fire was more destructive than theirs.

I am lying here under the impenetrable boughs of God's first temple, awaiting for some kind and benevolent hand to administer to my necessities. If I was near some rippling stream or gurgling spring, that I could quench my thirst, and bathe my wound in pure water, I would be all right, but I must be content with my condition until those are cared for that are in a worse condition than myself. I do not think of or grieve at my condition like I do for the dying ones around me. I lay here all night last night, and oh, what horror! Just think for a moment of the midnight groans of thousands dying in this wilderness far away from loved ones, their dying groans made more pitiful by the lonesome screaming of the whippowill and hooting owl.

The thought is too sad to contemplate. I can but think that your prayers in my behalf have been heard or I would have been launched unprepared into eternity, but through some great miraculous interposition of Providence I am spared, with a good prospect of soon being taken from this awful place to where the gentle hand of woman can soothe my fevered brow. This scene can never be obliterated from my memory.

I could be more resigned to my condition if I could be moved from the stench of the decaying bodies and pools of blood around me. My heart is filled with sympathy for the wounded Federals that are left on the field. Many of them are dying with thirst and exposure. I would to God that I could relieve them, but it is out of my power.

I will close for fear that I worry you with the detail of the awful scenes, but while I am writing to you it diverts my attention from the contemplation of my true condition. This is my excuse for worrying you. I will write you again soon and let you know where to direct your letters, when I am assigned to some hospital.

Hoping to hear from you soon, my dear one, I remain, as ever, your

ALBERT.

Albert sealed his letter and soon had a chance to send it off through the ambulance corps. After a short time he was taken from the field by some other soldiers who had been only slightly wounded and left on detail to nurse the helpless ones. Albert was taken to the field hospital, where his wound was dressed, and after a day and night's rest, he was sent by the ambulance to Orange Court House, where he took the train for Gordonsville; here he remained for two or three days, and was sent from there to Lynchburg. Along the route from Gordonsville to Lynchburg, Albert was feasted on every luxury that Virginia hospitality afforded. The ladies, who were so noted for their hospitality, were ready at every station on the road to administer to the want of the soldiers, to give them water and bathe their wounds and then pass around their delicacies, appearing to give them the most exquisite pleasure. Albert was so completely overcome with gratitude that he did not regret that he had left his native State and spilt his blood in defense of the homes of those lovely angels of mercy.

On May the 11th the sun rose in all the splendor necessary to make the mountain scenery near Lynchburg appear in all its magnificence and grandeur. The train was curving around the base of the small mountains so conspicuous along the road. While making those curves Albert had a good view of the beautiful valleys with their carpets of clover and grasses. All nature seemed to combine its attractions to make it the most lovely scene imaginable, as the cars went gliding across the James river and along its precipitous banks to the noisy city of Lynchburg, where he again met his rival.

XII

The Meeting

ALBERT'S RECEPTION at Lynchburg was such as could only be extended by fair women to a soldier who had been wounded in defense of his country.

The ladies of the city made it a part of the day's programme to be at the depot on the arrival of trains, to supply the sick and wounded with substantial food and delicacies—embracing ham, sandwiches, excellent bread and fresh butter, followed by cake, wine, strawberries, and the delicious mountain cherries for which that region is so justly celebrated.

While the ambulance corps was engaged in bearing the helpless human freight to the various hospitals, the ladies would crowd around the litters and minister to the comfort of the occupants, welcoming them to the city with sweet words of sympathetic sorrow that caused every sufferer to forget his ills, and made their hearts to throb with renewed hope and pleasure.

So many of the sick and wounded of the army of Northern Virginia had been already billeted upon the city, that almost all available room was occupied when Albert reached Lynchburg, and it was necessary to hastily put in order one of the immense tobacco factories, to accommodate those who could not be quartered in the regular hospital buildings. Albert was assisted into an ambulance and conveyed to the factory where he was placed on the edge of the sidewalk with his knapsack for a pillow, to await the erection of cots and bedding inside the house.

While he remained there many citizens, actuated by motives of curiosity and sympathy, passed and stopped to inquire after his wounds, and particulars of the great battle.

In looking around and about him, Albert noticed a soldier in the front door of the second story of the building. He knew the man must be a cavalryman by his plumed hat, high boots, big spurs and a long sabre hanging gracefully by his side. After watching him intently for some time, Albert was convinced that this was none other but Captain Winston, his rival and enemy, who had left Macon for Tennessee to join Morgan's cavalry at the same time Albert had left for Virginia. The Sixteenth battalion, to which Captain Winston belonged, had been sent to Lynchburg from Tennessee, to join General Imboden in checking the advance of the Federal, General Hunter, who was threatening that portion of Virginia. They were encamped in the outskirts of the city, and Albert supposed Captain Winston was looking through the hospitals to see if he could find friends or acquaintances, and was thus brought in close proximity to his rival. The Captain did not recognize Albert, as our hero's features were pale and haggard from suffering, and almost hidden in the smoke and dust of the bloody conflict he had just passed through, but when Albert called to him, and asked if he knew him, Captain Winston remembered his voice, and gazing down upon Albert with a look of scorn and contempt, not unmingled with pleasure at seeing his personal enemy in so bad a plight, the Captain replied:

"I suppose the Yankees have saved me the trouble of doing what you so richly deserve."

Albert replied:

"It is true I am wounded, sir, but whether I deserved to be or not, I leave to a higher power to determine."

Captain Winston made no reply, but stood for some time looking contemptuously down on his enemy with all the bad passions of his black and revengeful heart plainly reflected in his face. He finally turned from his position in the door, and slowly descending the steps he approached Albert's resting place under the shade on the sidewalk, as if he desired to fully enjoy his rival's unfortunate condition and make known the satisfaction he felt in crushing one who had aspired to the hand of the one he himself had sought to win.

After gloating his cruel eyes upon Albert's blood-stained clothing and pale ghastly features, he plainly showed his coarse, brutal nature during the following conversation:

CAPTAIN WINSTON: "Where are you from, and where did you receive that good shot at?"

ALBERT: "I am from Lee's army, and was wounded on the 6th instant."

CAPTAIN WINSTON: "I wish I could see the man that did it. I would not only thank, but I would give him some very tangible evidence of the joy I felt in seeing you in this condition."

ALBERT: "He was a soldier, like myself, and I do not suppose he desires either reward or thanks. If he survived the bloody engagement the satisfaction of having discharged his duty to himself and his country is the only recompense he deserves."

CAPTAIN WINSTON: "I thought you had deserted, and failed to join the army, as I did not hear from you."

ALBERT: "I suppose the wish was father to the thought.

And now that you have positive evidence to the contrary, your mind is unpleasantly disabused of such unjust suspicions."

CAPTAIN WINSTON: "Why did you not go to Tennessee, as you suggested?"

ALBERT: "Because some of the rairoads had been destroyed by the enemy, and communication stopped before I left Macon."

CAPTAIN WINSTON: "Don't you wish you had kept out of my way, and thus prevented a personal collision between us? If you had done so you would now have been in Georgia instead of lying here sick and wounded so far from home and friends."

ALBERT: "I did not get in your way intentionally, and never attempted to do you an injury except in self-defense. I would have killed you on one occasion, but for the interference of friends. I have thanked God often that I was prevented from shooting you, even though you had placed a pistol in my face with the determination to take my life. I would not have killed you for worlds, but only to preserve my own life."

CAPTAIN WINSTON: "If you were so anxious to avoid a difficulty, why did you place yourself between me and Florence?"

ALBERT: "Because I loved Florence, and she reciprocated it. She respected you as a friend only. She has promised to become my wife should I be so fortunate as to survive the casualties of war, and I intend to marry her or die in the attempt."

CAPTAIN WINSTON: "Then you are sure to die in the attempt, for I swear by the high Heaven you shall never claim her as your wife."

ALBERT: "You are not so heartless as to desire my death at the hands of the enemies of our country?"

CAPTAIN WINSTON: "Indeed I would, as it would spare me

the disagreeable duty of putting an end to your life, for should you survive the war, I have long since determined to kill you, unless you give up all idea of marrying Florence."

ALBERT: "That I will never do, unless she desires it, but I will not say that I desire to imbrue my hands in your blood. It would be a terrible duty for me to perform."

CAPTAIN WINSTON: "You lie! You would take my life now if you were physically able and I were in your power!"

Albert being wholly unable to defend himself made no reply, and Captain Winston soon turned away and left.

XIII

The Scales Turned

IT IS UNNECESSARY to follow Albert through the meandering scenes of the next few weeks after he was insulted by Captain Winston. Suffice it to say that by the time that a few weeks had passed he was sufficiently convalescent to return to his command for duty, but just about the time he was making ready to start, a body of raiders cut the line of communication between Lynchburg and Richmond. At the same time, Hunter, with twenty thousand men, was near at hand pressing down upon Lynchburg. General D. H. Hill had been placed in command of the Confederate forces around Lynchburg, consisting of the cavalry and a few militia. General Hill made an appeal to the wounded soldiers, calling on the ones that were able, to rendezvous at the convalescent camp near the city for the purpose of defending the homes of those fair ones who had nursed them and restored them to the service.

This call brought out every man who was sufficiently recovered to do duty, and in a few hours they were organized, armed and equipped, and proceeded to throw up breastworks around the city.

This little force, consisting of the convalescent, the

cavalry and militia, all combined did not exceed three thousand men. On the afternoon that Hunter made his appearance in front of this small band, it seemed that Lynchburg was to fall into his hands without a struggle. Had he only known the situation, he could have marched into the city with all ease; but the Confederate remnant opened a brisk fire on his advancing columns, causing him to halt, and he commenced to fortify himself, preparatory to a desperate struggle.

This bit of strategy on the part of the Confederates in deploying so as to extend their lines to a greater extent, deceived the Federal commander and saved Lynchburg. The city could have been taken that evening without the loss of a hundred men, but the Federals let the opportunity slip, and all night the trains were thundering into the city, bringing General Early's corps, which had been dispatched from Lee's army near Richmond. By dawn this gallant force, commanded by the daring Early, had taken its position in line and was ready to act on the aggressive instead of the defensive. At first daylight Early's veterans broke out in long and continued cheers and were joined by the other troops, making the hills and vales ring with the echoes, firing their hearts with enthusiasm and making the Federals tremble with fear. They knew they had lost the prize, and before sunrise Early had moved forward and the Federals retreated before the advancing Confederates, keeping up only a sufficient fire to protect their retreating columns.

This was the beginning of the memorable campaign of the valley. General Early pursued the Federals and forced them back upon their own capital, thus leaving Lynchburg and the surrounding country freed from the invaders.[15]

After this sharp, quick and decisive victory had been gained by the Confederates, and Early was driving the Federals out of the State, the convalescent troops were disbanded and sent back to their respective hospitals, and the cavalry to which Captain Winston belonged was ordered to move off in the direction of Maryland for the purpose of cutting off the communication of the enemy.

On the following day the ambulance corps went upon the field and moved all the wounded that could be found, leaving the dead to be buried on the next day. This disagreeable duty was to be performed on the Sabbath day by a detail of colored men, who were pressed into service by the city authorities, and when Albert saw them start off in the direction of the battle field with their picks and spades, he concluded to walk over to the scene of action, to look over the dead and see what could be found.

In a dense thicket of woodland about two miles from town was found a considerable number of bodies, left by the retreating enemy, and while the Negroes were gathering them up and placing them in a gully or ravine near by, Albert was busily engaged in searching over the ground for other matters of interest to him. Although the battle had been of short duration, it was of sufficient magnitude to make the scene of carnage a sickening one to behold. At intervals of a few paces could be found the body of a dead Federal, who had been robbed of nearly all his clothing by some heartless creatures who took a pleasure in robbing the dead. Broken guns and unsheathed sabres were scattered in every direction, with here and there a knapsack, a canteen or haversack, some of them lying in pools of human blood so conspicuous on every side. All served to make the scene a desolate one to behold on a quiet Sabbath day.

While Albert was going through the woods he came to a small branch and walked slowly along down the stream until he came in sight of a small field, in which was a slight eminence. Upon this the enemy had built a small fortress, which was a square embankment of dirt, thrown up to protect a light battery. Here the Confederate cavalry had made a charge with success. In making this charge the cavalry had to cross a fence that ran parallel with another small stream that made a connection with the stream before mentioned. In the fork of this branch near the battery Albert found a horse lying with his head doubled up under his body—a grape shot from the cannon had pierced a hole though the neck, killing him instantly, causing him in his fall to plunge forward, doubling his head under his body and throwing the rider head foremost to the ground.

Albert stood for a moment, staring at the dead beast, thinking of what a fearful shock the fall must have given the rider. While thus meditating, he raised his head and looked in the direction the horse had been going when he met with this unhappy fate, and just beyond the fence near the bank of the stream he perceived what he thought to be a dead cavalryman. Albert approached the fence, and looking over saw that the man was not dead. He stood a moment gazing at the body to make sure it was breathing. After satisfying himself that the soldier still lived, he crossed the fence, walked up to where the man was lying, and to his surprise he looked into the face of Captain John Winston.

Such a haggard, miserable face Albert never had seen before. His heart great faint and sick, and he could scarcely refrain from shedding tears. Captain Winston had been thrown by the fall of his horse while making the charge; yet after recovering from the fall he rose up and with sabre in hand, pressed forward toward the battery. While crossing the fence a Federal sharp-shooter singled him out, and with unerring aim, lodged a "minnie"* ball in his breast, which cut through the left lung and lodged in his body. The litter corps had left him on the field as dead when they were

*Named for its inventor, Captain Minie, in 1847.

hunting up the wounded, and in this manner he had been lying for three days and nights without food or water. While the water was so near him that he could hear the gurgling sounds as it rippled along, he could not get a drop to cool his parched lips or quench his burning thirst. Here in his agony he had prayed for death, and if he could have gotten a weapon he would have terminated his own existence with pleasure. When Albert approached him, the Captain looked up and recognized him.

"Captain Winston!" cried Albert, "Captain Winston, can I do anything for you, sir?"

This seemd to mortify Captain Winston's feelings so much that he turned his head from Albert and replied, feebly: "I am in your power at last; take my life if you wish, but please don't mortify my feelings with things of the past. I must die soon and I don't wish to be burdened with bygones."

Albert answered: "I have buried the past, Captain Winston, and if you will let me help you, it would be the greatest pleasure of my life to relieve your suffering. May I give you a drink of water and bathe your wound?"

"Oh, Albert! How dare I to take a drink of water from your hands, or receive a favor of any kind from one who would be glad to take my life?"

Albert, without waiting for him to finish his scattering and almost incoherent remarks, stooped down into the branch and dipped up some water on the brim of his hat, and raising Captain Winston's head with one hand, poured the cooling liquid into his mouth.

The Captain then realized that Albert was in earnest in desiring to relieve his pain, and he was so overcome with gratitude that he could no longer restrain his feelings, and the hot, burning tears began to roll down his cheeks.

XIV

The Reconciliation

ALBERT SAT DOWN by Captain Winston, and taking the officer's head in his lap, began to unbutton his collar to examine the wound. He found that the ball, in entering the breast, had driven the shirt into the wound made by the deadly missile, and this had checked, to a certain extent, the flow of blood. Albert pulled the cloth from the wound, which started a flow of bruised blood, and that gave a considerable relief to the sufferer. After using a soldier's remedy for wounds, which was invariably a bath in cold water, Albert took from his pocket a stained handkerchief and wiped the blood from the wound. Then dipping the handkerchief in the branch, he folded it and laid it on the wound for the purpose of cooling the fever.

The cool water that Albert poured into his mouth and the bathing of his wounds had such a soothing effect that Captain Winston could not resist the spell that came over him, and before Albert was through dressing the wound, he had dropped into a gentle slumber.

Albert went back to where they were burying the dead, and sent one of the colored men back to the city for an ambulance to convey Captain Winston to the city.

On returning to where the Captain was, Albert found him still asleep, so he took a seat beside him and began to drive the flies from the wounds by fanning them with a bunch of green leaves plucked from a tree near by. While thus engaged, he heard Captain Winston begin to mutter about something which seemed to trouble him in his dreams. His struggles awoke him, and he saw Albert sitting over him, watching him with an eye of tenderness. Looking Albert in the face, he said, "Ah, Albert, I have at last learned your true character. I dreamed you had put poison in the water you gave me, and it caused me to wake and find you sitting over me, trying to comfort me like a mother. How can I thank you, my dear friend, for your kindness?"

Albert replied, "I am entitled to no thanks; it is a duty we all owe to each other, and to relieve your suffering and restore your manhood and vigor would be my greatest pleasure."

"You can quench my thirst and ease my wound temporarily," said Winston, "but it is out of your power to benefit me permanently, for death has already put its own seal upon me. I thank you, not because I think you will save my life, but I thank you because you have forgiven me. I am led to believe that if you, who I so cruelly treated, can forgive me, my Savior, who is more merciful, will do likewise. To receive your forgiveness is a great relief to me, and will comfort me while I am struggling with the awful pangs of death. I have lived over my life again since I received this, my death wound, and the remorse I have felt in consequence of my treatment of you, no mortal tongue can express. The manner in which I treated you when you were prostrate at my feet, suffering from your wound, has given me the keenest pangs of regret. I had previously injured you, and then added insult to injury by speaking harsh to you when you were helpless."

"Don't say any more," responded Albert, "for as I told you, I have buried the past. I will not allude to the subject again if you desire it. Your condition is bad enough without having your feelings mortified by talking of things that are unpleasant to you."

"Ah, Albert, it is not unpleasant to me, since I have learned that you have forgiven me. I know that I am compelled to die, and it was a horrible thought to me that I would be wafted into eternity without a reconciliation with you. But now that I am assured that you are worthy of the hand of Florence, and that you have forgiven me for the manner in which I treated you about the dear sweet girl, I can die with but one regret, and that is because I will never live to meet Florence again, and ask her pardon for the manner in which I treated her. I loved her so rudely that I allowed the infatuation to dethrone my reason. I had not told her of my love until I learned that she loved you, and then I became desperate. I did not know that I loved her so dearly until I learned that she was loved by another. Then I felt that life without her would be a misery to me. I could not bear the thought of ever seeing her the wife of another. I knew that she did not love me, but I believed that she would grow to love me. Until I was convinced that you had gained the prize that I sought, I could not live and see her sweet smiles and tender affections bestowed upon another. Consequently I acted on the impulse, and yielded to the dictates of my worst passions, and you know the result. If you could only know the pangs that I have felt, you would sympathize with me, but I hope your manly and noble heart will never feel such pangs of jealousy, or see the idol of your heart won by another—you will never know until you love as I have loved, and see the object of your affections treat the same with contempt, and bestow the most tender smiles upon another. Had I but made known to Florence the sentiments of love to which she had inspired me before you met her, perhaps it would have been different. She admired me as a friend, and had she only known how dearly I loved her, perhaps her admiration would have ripened into reciprocal love. But alas, it is too late now to repair the great wrong that I have done her. If I could only have the pleasure of one last interview with her and tell her how I feel towards her! If I could only explain to her my true feelings towards you, now, perhaps she, like you, would throw the mantle of charity over my faults and forgive me for all the wrongs that I have done, ere I pass from earth to the Bar of final judgment, where I will have One to intercede for me who knows all the weakness of mortal man, and through His tender mercies I hope to receive a reward of ultimate glory."

"Perhaps you are not so near death as you think, Captain Winston," replied Albert, "You know that you are considerably revived since I gave you water to drink and bathed your wound, and when the ambulance arrives, and you are carried to the city where you will get nourishments from the hands of fair ones, you may soon be well and live long to thank them for their tender and hospitable treatment. You remember when you saw me last I was lying on the pavement in the city, clothed in blood-stained garments, but now see me restored to health and doing my duty by trying to relieve the sufferings of you, my fellow creature."

XV

Friends

CAPTAIN WINSTON: "Ah, Albert, you mortify me by alluding to the insult you received at my hands when you were prostrate at my feet, clad in tattered blood-stained garments, suffering from a wound received while nobly defending our sunny South. I regret that insult more than anything that has occurred in the course of the unhappy affair between us. When I put the pistol in your face on the Southwestern Railroad,* with the intention to kill you, I was in a dreadful passion, and you had an equal chance with me, consequently my conscience does not chide me about that incident as it does about the brutal insult I gave you when you were helpless."

ALBERT: "I did not refer to my wound and that meeting with you, to mortify you, Captain Winston, but to encourage you in the hope that the kind treatment you will receive in the hospital at the hands of the surgeons and the noble hearted women will so far restore you as to allow you to return to Georgia on furlough, when you will be able to see

* Route from Macon to Andersonville; town named for president of the road, John W. Anderson.

Florence and tell her all, and be friends again, if she will accept your apology. As for your attempt to shoot me, I did not think much of it, for I knew that you acted hastily and without due consideration, and I doubtless acted a little hastily myself in accusing you of intercepting my letters to Florence. I was sincere in my belief. Yet, be that as it may, when you sent me a challenge to meet you outside the city limits, in mortal combat, I knew you had not reflected upon the consequences that might ensue. Hence, I preferred to defer a hostile meeting until the end of the war, in order to give you time to think over the affair calmly and dispassionately, become better acquainted with my true character, and conclude to dismiss all revengeful feelings from your heart. I knew very well that a duel between us would result in death to both of us, as one of us would have been killed at the hands of the other, and the survivor court martialed and shot."

Captain Winston: "Oh, no, Albert, I will never return to Georgia on furlough. I can live but a few hours at the fartherest—my wound is fatal. I do not hope to live, and could I only see Florence and ask and receive her forgiveness for the unhappiness I have caused her, I would not even desire to live, but resign her future happiness to your keeping with the sincere hope that you both might realize, in each other's society, the full fruition of your hopes."

Just as Captain Winston had finished speaking, the colored man arrived who had been sent to bring the ambulance which had been left on the turnpike near the toll-gate, and with Albert's assistance the wounded man was carried to the vehicle on a litter, placed in it as comfortably as possible, and conveyed to the hospital, where he received the attention he so much needed. For some days Captain Winston seemed to improve rapidly, and during this time Albert visited him regularly, sat by his cot and read the morning papers to him, which he always carried for that purpose, and did everything in his power to assist his former rival to submit to his sufferings with a cheerful spirit. They would discuss each situation from all points, after reading the news, and speculate upon the probable issue of the campaign.

Albert had concluded that the Captain would most certainly recover, but to his surprise on entering the hospital one morning, he discovered a pool of blood on the floor under Captain Winston's bed, and a surgeon trying to stop the hemorrhage of the wound in the Captain's breast, which had bled so freely that the blood had soaked through the mattress and stood in a clotted mass or puddle on the floor. As Albert approached him he raised his head and looked imploring into his face, as much as to say, "Help me if you can." Albert knew from the quiver of his pale and bloodless lips that the man was in great agony, and for the first time he felt powerless to give any relief.

After considerable effort, the surgeon succeeded in checking the flow of blood, temporarily, but he told his patient that it was beyond his power to stop it long, and that the next flow would be all he could stand. Being thus assured of his real condition, the Captain asked the surgeon to write down his name, age, company, regiment, state and county, and asked him to mark his grave after he was buried, and also to write to his parents in Georgia and inform them of his death.

After all the routine of duties in the hospital had been performed for the night, and the nurses had taken their places by the side of the most critical cases of the wounded to watch them, Albert retired to his own quarters for rest. He had now lost all hope of Captain Winston's recovery, and consequently was very sad, and felt much grief when thinking of the unpleasant feeling that once existed between him and the dying man. The thoughts that pressed upon his mind kept him from sleep, and when he had worried till overcome by want of rest, he dozed off and did not wake until late next morning. As soon as he could get ready, his first thought was to see Captain Winston, and upon entering the room he beheld his lifeless body lying with his hands folded across his breast and a sheet thrown over his face. Albert raised the sheet and looked into the cold and expressionless face of his rival, his friend. Like a flash of lightning his mind reverted to the past, and so vivid did each sad scene present itself, he could no longer restrain his feelings, and turned from the corpse, his cheeks burning with tears. As Albert was turning away, the master of the eleventh ward approached him and told him the particulars of the death. He informed Albert that Captain Winston had called him to his bedside during the night and requested him to write a letter for him, with request that it be shown to Albert before being sealed. Handling the letter to Albert he turned and walked off. Albert read the address, which was "Miss Florence ———, Macon, Ga." He opened it with a trembling hand, and read as follows:

IN HOSPITAL, LYNCHBURG, VA.
June ——th, 1864

MISS FLORENCE: Mortified and Injured Friend—As this is my last day on earth, I hope you will pardon me for intruding upon your feelings by sending you a few lines, written for me by a friend. I would not intrude upon your time but for to ask your forgiveness for the trouble that I have been instrumental in giving you in the past. I need not tell you all, but it will be sufficient for you to know that Albert, the noble hearted boy that you loved so well, has pardoned me, and I hope you will not be less charitable than your lover. I hope it will be some comfort to you to know that I have found him to be the most noble hearted man that ever lived. Had it not been for him, I should have died on the battle field without ever having an opportunity of asking your pardon—the only prize that I now desire on Earth. This you surely cannot deny to a dying man. When Albert returns home he will tell you all. Should he be so fortunate as to survive the war, I hope he will make you as happy as I have made you miserable. I acknowledge the error that I committed in attempting to take the life of as fine a boy as ever lived, and thereby crushing the hopes of as lovely a creature as ever bloomed into womanhood, and I hope you will be as willing to pardon my faults as I am to acknowledge them, which is all that I can do.

It is out of my power to return your lover to you, although I was the cause of his leaving you, but he will return to you unchanged unless he, like myself, is numbered with the slain before this unholy war is terminated. When that will be, God only knows, and I will never know, for when this reaches you I will be lying in the cold clay numbered with the millions that have gone before me. All my earthly hopes have been like a bubble on the ocean—they glittered and dazzled for a moment and then flitted away, and are no more. May the frail bark of life waft you down the stream of time, until you glide into the broad ocean of eternal happiness. This is the prayer of your dying friend,

JOHN WINSTON

XVI

Returned to the Front

ALBERT READ Winston's letter and returned it to the Ward Master with the request to allow him to copy it before mailing. The request being granted, he left the room and visited the various other hospitals in the city to enquire after the condition of other wounded friends. After a few hours he returned to Ward No. 11 and found that the body of Captain Winston had been removed to the dead-house, there to remain until the arrival of a load of coffins and the time for the dray to make its regular daily trip to the soldiers' cemetery. Hence, Albert never knew where the grave of Captain Winston was. He only knew that the remains were sent to the burial place with other bodies and there rudely interred, to remain until the Resurrection Day, unless taken by friends or relatives to Georgia and re-interred in the soil of his Mother State.

Soon after the death of Captain Winston, communication was reestablished between Lynchburg and Richmond by the repairing of the railroad near Burkeville junction. As soon as this was done, the trains were crowded every day with soldiers returning to their command. Then on one of those hot July days, our hero made his way back to the front to join his comrades in the trenches around Richmond and Petersburg, in that great struggle around the Confederate Capital. On arriving at the Capital, he learned that his regiment was in line on the south side of the James, near Petersburg. He stopped for the night in Richmond, where he witnessed some heart rending scenes such as the amputating of legs and arms of the soldiers who were continually arriving from the ditches with shattered limbs and bleeding wounds.

During the entire night, the roar of cannon could be heard all along the lines, which extended from the Weldon railroad on the south of Petersburg, to the James, and across to the north side of Richmond, a distance of twenty-five or forty miles. The large guns at Drewry's bluff, that kept up a continual fire on the working force of Beast Butler in Dutch Gap canal[16] made the buildings in the city tremble like a distant earthquake. Many readers can recall to mind those nights of horror, when the elements were ablaze with flying shells and flashing cannon, interspersed with the clatter of musketry, as the sharp-shooters and pickets endeavored to pick off the artillery men as they loaded and fired the cannon.

After one of those horrible nights spent in Richmond, Albert boarded the train for his command and in a short time sped into the city of Petersburg amidst screaking shot, bursting shells, tumbling walls and flying brickbats. None but those who have witnessed such scenes can form an idea of its horrors. On every side was the wildest excitement. In one place the city was on fire, and as the firemen approached the conflagration the enemy sent a shower of iron hail from their batteries, so destructive that the firemen were compelled to seek shelter in the cellars of the shattered buildings. The ladies who had not left the city were weeping and running to and fro, seeking refuge in the upper part of the city, while others took shelter in their gardens where they had prepared for the worst by digging holes in the ground and covering them with timber and dirt, thus forming what the soldiers called bomb-proofs.

As the trains would pass in and out of the city, the batteries would open fire on them and create a panic among the passengers who were leaving the city.

On an elevated position one mile from the suburbs of the city was an enemy battery that did so much damage the citizens gave it the name of Fort Hell. Many ex-Confederates will recall to mind the gas works and vicinity, and the suburban village of Pocahontas, which were literally riddled by the destructive battery.[17]

Albert, having met an old friend who was on detail in consequence of having been disabled in battle, learned from him the condition of the company to which he belonged. He informed Albert that after leaving the Wilderness, the company suffered heavily in the battles of Spottsylvania Court House, Turkey Ridge, Jericho Ford, Cold Harbor and Ridley's [Riddell's] Shop, and the remnant of the company were then in the trenches near Fort Clifton, numbering only a handful of men, about a Corporal's guard.[18] The veteran also informed him that many of his old friends in the other companies from Butts county were killed and wounded. Among them, an old schoolmate had lost an arm at Cold Harbor, and another friend and associate had lost a leg by the explosion of a shell while lying in the trenches near Petersburg. Still another one was brained while sharp-shooting over the breast-works with the enemy. The sad tidings of the death of so many dear friends and relatives almost unnerved our hero and caused him to feel that the cause they had sacrificed so much blood and treasure to defend, would be hopelessly lost. But as all dark clouds cease to be frightful when a brilliant streak of light breaks forth behind them, so it was with Albert when he called at the post office and received a dainty letter that had been forwarded from

Lynchburg, and was post-marked "Macon, Ga." This welcome visitor, like all the letters received from Florence, was full of pledges of devotion to her lover, and the cause for which he battled. The hope of gaining the victory at last in the final struggle and securing Southern independence caused all fear to banish from the thoughts of our hero, and with the encouraging words of Florence fresh in his memory, he pressed forward through the confusion until he reached the trenches where the remnant of his company was, whereupon he heard the men cry out, "Albert's come, Albert's come!"

XVII

The Siege at Petersburg

AFTER THE greeting that Albert received at the hands of his comrades, he resumed his position in ranks with cheerfulness and alacrity, and did all in his power to relieve his fatigued and careworn companions by doing picket duty in rotation for each one of them.

The continued firing along the line worried him very much at first, but after a few days he began to feel more at ease, and even while lying under the burning rays of a July sun, or chilled by the tidewater breeze at night, he remained cheerful and content. Many a jest was gotten off at the expense of some weary rebel, who in turn would get up something at the expense of his adversary.

Things moved on in this way for several days after Albert's return to camps, until the 30th of July, when the entire Confederate force was wrapped in slumber except those on duty on the picket line. Just at daylight they were roused from their slumbers by a sudden convulsion like an earthquake, followed by a rumbling noise like a volcano on the eve of an eruption. The wildest excitement prevailed. The query, "What is the matter?" was heard on every side, and before any explanation of this terrible explosion could be had, the report of a fearful volley of musketry was heard on the right, followed by wild and repeated *huzzahs* in the Federal lines, which fully explained the shocking noise. General Grant had fired a powder mine and blown up a rebel battery. This was done by tunneling for two hundred yards and placing a quantity of powder (which we afterwards learned amounted to eight thousand pounds), under the rebel lines, and when directly under a battery the train was fired by means of a fuse. Grant hoped this explosion would cause a panic in the vicinity of the mine, which he hoped to take advantage of to break the Confederate line and march his hosts triumphantly into the city of Petersburg. It had the desired effect. The panic stricken Confederates retreated in confusion and left that part of the line open to the advancing Federals, but before the Federals could press on to the city and take possession of it, the Confederates had recovered from their fright, and with their usual courage and heroism, rallied and charged upon the captured works. One of the fiercest and bloodiest hand to hand conflicts of the war then occurred.

The Federal commander ordered a division of colored troops into the pit caused by the explosion of the mine, and when the rebels charged upon them they fell like straws before the wind—several hundred being covered with dirt and left in the pit after the battle.

During the time the struggle was going on, troops were being drawn from all parts of the line and concentrated near the scene of action, but before their services were needed the Confederates, who had been driven from their position, had recaptured the works, along with more than a thousand prisoners, and killed and wounded more men than were engaged on their own side. Thus ended the most stupendous scene that has been conceived in modern warfare, after which the troops resumed their positions in line, and everything was silent except the reverberations of the siege guns and the echo of the never ceasing sharp-shooting.

The seige around Richmond and Petersburg lasted nine months after Albert's arrival. We could write volumes on the incidents through which our hero passed, but one incident in particular illustrates the cause of the devotion of Lee's men to their noble commander.

In the latter part of the summer or fall of 1864, a part of Grant's army had been massed and a successful charge made against the Weldon Railroad just south of Petersburg. A counter charge by the Confederates had been successful to the extent of re-capturing the railroad, but had not pushed Grant's troops back far enough to re-capture all of the lost ground. Part of the rebel forces were engaged in throwing up new breastworks between the railroad and the position then held by the enemy. Albert was helping in the work.

Near the old gas works a citizen had a two or three-acre patch of corn in roasting ear. General Lee ordered a guard to watch over that corn night and day to protect the citizen's property.

Goaded by that craving feeling that every old soldier remembers, that comes to one who has not had his appetite satisfied for weeks past, Albert decided to risk the bullet of the guard and the punishment of army discipline in the determination to get some of that corn.

Leaving the workers for a short time, he made his way through the thick undergrowth and over the fence and secured two roasting ears. Returning along a path through the undergrowth he stopped, struck a match, collected leaves and twigs and made a small fire.

Having removed the shuck, he soon had the two ears of corn standing on end baking one side at the time, by the coals. He was stooping to turn them, when he heard a horse walking behind him. Turning around—great heavens! General Lee had brought "Traveler" to a standstill, while he sat there like a statue.

Now every old veteran that reads this will know exactly what the boy expected—to be ordered to headquarters for punishment. But that noble old Roman did nothing of the sort.

With his face all wreathed in smiles, he looked first into the youth's frightened countenance, and then at the corn, and with a slight pressure of the bridle-rein with the left hand, causing "Traveler" to slightly sway to the left, with his right hand he gave the most graceful salute our hero had ever seen. In return Albert gave him the most grateful, though not the most graceful one, he would ever give.

The grand old hero pulled his horse from the path, a sad expression passed over his face, and he said, "My poor boys are starving."

Albert ate the half-cooked roasting ears and with appetite partially satisfied, went back to work, determined to stand by General Lee until death.

Often, in all the years to come he would ask himself, "Did I do wrong? Did General Lee do wrong?" His conscience would answer, "no." And he knew the man who owned that corn would also answer "no."

Lee had the power to punish and the power to pardon. When the final history of that great struggle is written, Albert hoped something of this incident would be remembered as an inspiration to those in authority in ages to come. He would always feel the incident made him a better man in after years, as it taught him not to condemn his fellow man until he knew what prompted the act.

Many more things occurred, but it will be sufficient for the reader to know that Albert witnessed everything connected with the memorable siege. Many days and nights were spent in dirt and filth, in rifle pits that would have answered for a grave, and many days were spent lying in the breast-works exposed to the scorching rays of a summer's sun and the pitiless winter storms of rain, snow and sleet, scantily fed and thinly clad and subject to contract one of the many diseases an army is subject to. Many forced marches were also made to repel the frequent flank movements and reconnoitering parties of the enemy in his attempts to get possession of the Weldon R.R., south of Petersburg, or the Gordonsville R.R., on the north side of Richmond.[19]

One evening while on his way to the pits Albert noticed a well-laden hickory tree not too far back. Wishing to supplement his rather meager rations he decided that it would be safe to go back for some nuts. The other members of the group tried to dissuade him, saying that there was a rather dangerous sharp-shooter just across the river. Hunger, however, prevailed over better judgment, and he crouched low as he left the pit, and almost fell back into it as he noted a small puff of smoke across the river and heard a bullet whack into a near by tree. Judgment, this time, prevailed over hunger!

The saddest sight witnessed by our hero during the siege was the little children roaming the streets begging for bread, while meal was selling at one hundred and twenty-five dollars per bushel, and meat fifteen dollars per pound, and flour nine hundred dollars per barrel. Incredible as this may appear, it is nevertheless true, and those who are familiar with the facts can easily account for the downfall of the Confederacy and the subsequent poverty of the conquered states.

Many times during the long restless nights spent in the ditches, our hero would gaze at the twinkling stars and think of home, sweet home, and loved ones, and long for peace to dawn upon his unhappy country. The letters received from

Florence and friends indicated a sad state of affairs in Georgia. Atlanta had fallen, and Hood, with his shattered army, had abandoned the State to the mercy of the invaders and gone in the direction of Tennessee, leaving Sherman an unobstructed pathway for a triumphal march to the sea.

When Albert learned that his native State was to be subjected to the long train of horrors that follow the course of an invading army, he would often look away to the southwest and imagine he could see the smoke of the burning buildings in the track of the victorious army. Thus it was that the army of Northern Virginia became discouraged by the failure of the Western army which, notwithstanding the splended fighting material of which it was composed, was forced to yield to superior numbers.

The defeat of this army had a very depressing effect upon General Lee's forces, and the winter of '64 passed monotonously with the exception of the charge on Fort Harrison, the capture and recapture of the Weldon R.R., the capture and recapture of Fort Hell, etc.

The monotonous sound of the bombardment of Petersburg, and the ceaseless picket firing did not lull until about the first of April '65, when the movements of the Federal commander indicated a policy which, if successful, would make an era in the history of modern warfare.

XVIII

Lost in Battle

ON THE MORNING of the 25th of March, the rebel officers learned that large bodies of the enemy were moving off in the direction of the Southside R.R. for the purpose of cutting off all communication southward and thus starve the hungry Confederates into a surrender.

The time for the final struggle had now arrived, as the enemy had determined to take possession of the last railroad left to supply the besieged army.

This movement made it necessary for the Confederates either to withdraw from their fortifications and fight the enemy one to ten in the open field, or else attack them in their works in front of the city, with the view of breaking their lines where they had been weakened by the withdrawal of troops for the flank movements. Of the two alternatives, General Lee chose the latter, and during the night of the 25th the available force of his army was concentrated in front of the city, and the picket was ordered to crawl up in front of the enemy's works and pull up the *abattie**, preparatory to a charge at daylight.

---

* *Abatis:* an obstruction of felled trees, with the branches sharpened and pointed in the direction of expected attack. In this case, the Rebel picket is removing the enemy's abatis.

When the time for the charge had arrived, the column moved forward to a successful charge and took possession of the enemy's works.

This splendid manoeuvre resulted so favorably that the Confederates, elated with the partial success, failed to wait for further orders and without making any halt in captured works, pressed forward up the hill, and before the enemy's surprised artillery men could dress themselves and man their guns, the victorious rebels rushed into Fort Hell and took the garrison prisoners. But right at this juncture the Confederates made an awful blunder—the troops who had been left to support the charging column failed to come up and occupy the captured works, and while the advancing column was taking possession of Fort Hell, the enemy came up on the breast-works from the right and left and cut off the entire force in the Fort, thus turning a brilliant victory into a disastrous defeat to the Confederates, in which they lost about three thousand prisoners.

While this engagement was going on, the Federals concluded to return the compliment by trying the rebel lines two miles to the right, near Battery No. 45.

The loss of so many prisoners at Fort Hell was a heavy blow to the Confederates and made it appear that the assaults of the enemy near Battery 45 could not be repulsed. But the deadly fire of the cannon, charged to their fullest capacity with canister and grape, began to cut gaps in the well-dressed columns of the advancing boys in blue, causing them to waver and recede to the cover of a hill where they reinforced for a more desperate struggle.

During this short cessation of the strife, the division to which Albert belonged was ordered to move at a double-quick to the field that was soon to be bathed in blood, amidst the thunder of cannon, the rattle of musketry, canopied by the smoke of battle. This was perhaps the grandest display

Cartography by Karen McHaney from contemporary maps, courtesy of the National Archives and Records Service, Cartographic Branch, Washington, D. C.

Petersburg Area, 1864–1865.

made during the war—the long line of Confederates moving at a right-oblique in double-quick time, while the Federal troops were moving upon the field in massed columns with a steady tread and a firm resolution. As every shrub or tree had been cut and burned, both armies could be seen distinctly as they moved on to battle. The Confederates arrived in the second line of works just in time to see the enemy charge the first line and pour over into the works and capture the rebels that were in them. This temporary success brought forth a wild *huzzah* from the victorious Federals, waving their banners defiantly at the brave Confederates, who returned the salute with a yell that sent a thrill of terror to the enemy.

Just at that moment a courier dashed along the lines with orders to sling canteens and haversacks, and prepare for a charge. At the command, "Forward!" the rebels moved across the open field and routed the enemy from the captured works, which were again recaptured.

During this strife both armies were badly cut up; each in turn suffered defeat, and after a day's hard fighting both armies had lost many—killed, wounded and captured.

That night the Confederates were called up in line for roll call, each company desiring to learn who had been killed, etc., each one of the men being requested to answer for his missing comrades.

When the roll of the company to which Albert belonged was called, Albert's name being called, his voice could not be heard in answer, and as was customary when a name of one who was lost was pronounced, silence of a moment ensued. A member of the company answered, "Albert's killed."

XIX

Florence

NOW, DEAR READER, we will turn to the dear, sweet girl who had been the innocent cause of the strife between the rival lovers, and give you a brief sketch of the final termination of the love affair between her and our hero. If we were writing a novel, and were to follow the inclination of our fancy, we would tell you that Florence and Albert were married after the struggle was over; but as we are only writing facts connected with one of the many sad incidents of the late war between the States, we must stick to facts and tell you that Florence and Albert never realized their fond hopes of matrimonial bliss, but like thousands and thousands of other young men and ladies, both North and South, their fondest hopes were blighted by the cruel hand of death.

Many a reader will recall to mind the sad disappointments and can yet feel the pang of hopes blighted by future happiness being crushed. Yea, many indeed were the pledges of devotion given with the parting hand, as the young and valiant soldiers of both sections went forth to a discharge of what they considered their most sacred duty, with a bouyant hope of returning to claim a merited reward, but were either slain in battle or cut down by some of the fatal diseases that camp life is subject to. And also many that passed through all the vicissitudes of war returned to find that the idol of their heart had been taken by the grim monster Death, thus crushing long cherished hopes of future happiness.

Florence yielded to all the sorrows and trials of the war with a Christian resignation, and did all in her power to cheer Albert by writing him constantly and picturing to him the brightest side for the future.

She wept bitterly when she received Albert's letter written while lying on the battle field wounded, but after her feeling of anguish had moderated, she wrote Albert in answer to his letter, and with those sentiments characteristic of a true Southern girl, did much to restore him to health and duty, for the best remedy for a wounded soldier was to drive away despondency. This Florence's letters never failed to do, as she was one of those rare beings who live to make others happy instead of miserable. Although she had lived to see the noble old State of Georgia pillaged by an invading army, and many homes burned, helpless women insulted, people driven from their homes to beg or starve, and some sections of the State almost depopulated, yet she never wrote despondingly to Albert.

She received the tidings of Captain Winston's death with sadness, and as much as she had been shocked by his conduct, she felt deeply mortified at his untimely death, and regretted very much that she could not see him and grant pardon before he died. She was too noble to rejoice at the death of the Captain, although she believed that he stood between her and future happiness.

Florence spent much of her time in visiting the wounded in the hospitals of Macon, carrying them nourishments of various kinds. Receiving their kindest thanks made her feel that she had discharged her duty and reciprocated the kindness of some of Virginia's fair daughters who had done so much to relieve the sufferings of her lover.

After each battle Florence would be very restless until she would receive a letter from Albert. The time passed wearily with her—hours were like days, and days like weeks, until she could learn of his condition. As the newspapers always published the casualities of each regiment, she would search the papers over time and again to learn the fate of her loved one, and when she found the list of casualities of the regiment to which he belonged, she would shrink with horror while reading the list of killed for fear that Albert's name would be found numbered with the slain.

During those days of horrible suspense, if she received a letter backed in Albert's hand writing, she would press it to her lips and soil it with tears before opening it.

After the battle in which Albert was lost, Florence failed to receive any letter and became very restless and uneasy, and sent to the post office at every mail time with the hope of receiving something from Albert, but in vain. As she was not of a desponding nature, she formed many excuses for not receiving a letter. As Sherman had passed into the Carolinas, she concluded that perhaps they had cut the railroad, and thus stopped communication and prevented letters passing south from Richmond.

Things moved on in this way until Florence received a paper with the list of casualties of Albert's regiment. Her gaze drifted down the columns until she found the list of killed. Glancing over it she caught sight of the name of Albert—and with a scream, she dropped the paper and fell senseless to the floor.

XX

The Frail Flower

FLORENCE'S MOTHER rushed to her side and raised the senseless form in her arms, and with the assistance of the servants conveyed her to a quiet resting place, where she soon returned to her consciousness.

Her mother was not aware of the fact that Florence had received the paper that brought the sad tidings which crushed her hopes, and could not account for her fainting until she kissed the girl and said, "Tell me, dear, what is the matter?"

Florence gazed wildly around, as if she scarcely knew where she was or what was wrong; but as soon as she could collect her thoughts sufficiently to realize her condition, she pointed to the paper on the floor and exclaimed, "Oh, Mother! It's too bad! I can't stand it! Oh, my Albert, my Albert! They have killed him! They have killed him!"

She then burst into passionate sobs, mingled with pitiful mourning and weeping. Her mother understood it all then. She knew that Florence had learned through the papers that Albert, her intended husband, had been killed in battle. She knew that to talk to her now would add to her grief and decided to let her weep until her aching heart would find relief in the flow of tears.

Charging the servant to watch over her daughter, she left Florence and returned to her own room with a heavy heart.

What would she not then have given to comfort her idolized daughter! The thought that her pretty child with her soft innocent eyes and smooth glossy hair would perhaps wilt under her sorrow, as the flower fadeth when severed from the stem, touched the tenderest cords of her heart, and caused her to weep bitterly. She loved her sweet girl with all the tenderness of a mother's love, and as Florence loved Albert so devotedly, she had hoped that he would make her his wife, but now she felt that the hopes of her dear daughter were blighted and her prospects of happiness gone forever. She could hardly realize the change of that innocent face but a few moments since as blithe and cheerful as a pure conscience and a happy heart could make it, now changed into mute, tearful agony. She knew that it would be a great struggle for Florence to give up her idolized lover, for whom she would gladly have sacrificed life itself to promote his happiness.

After weeping and meditating for some time, she returned to Florence's room and found her still weeping, but not so passionately. Seeing that Florence had begun to become more reconciled she entered into conversation with her with the view of diverting her mind from the subject by talking of other matters, but Florence would not, could not, think of anything else.

When the time for tea had arrived, her mother tried to get Florence to take some nourishments, but could not get her to eat anything.

As she could not get her daughter's mind drawn from the subject, she concluded to persuade her that it might not be so bad after all: perhaps there is some mistake; Albert may not be killed, although the report is official; or if he is killed, weeping will not do any good and he is no better favored than thousands of others that have been killed in the same cause, and while it is natural for us to grieve for them, we must bow submissively to fate, and forget our sorrows, and instead of weeping for the slain, should forget the past and live to make the living more happy. Now, if Albert is gone, you can find another who is worthy of the prize he sought and soon forget your past love. . . .

This was too much for Florence. The bare thought of forgetting Albert gave her intense agony, and with the deepest emotion, she replied, "Oh, dear Mama, how can you expect me to forget one who was so noble and pure hearted, one who would bear all the wrongs of the world rather than do an injury to another. If I could have died instead of him, and he been spared to live to accomplish noble deeds, it would have been far better, but I am left to weep and sigh for long years, and perhaps never know where his precious dust is resting. Perhaps he fell like the young South Carolinian that he wrote about, who was killed at the Wilderness; or worse still, perhaps he, like Captain Winston, was left on the battle field for dead, but with sufficient life left to feel the torture of dying with thirst, hunger and despair. It is too bad, too bad. Will I never know his fate? If I could have only been by his side, and pillowed his head on my arm and bathed his brow as the hot blood trickled from his heart, he could have died in peace, and I could have submitted to giving him up to the silent tomb. But the thought of his being cut off without a dying prayer, or a thought of me, is more than a human heart can bear."

She no longer tried to restrain her tears, but with wringing hands and aching heart dropped her head on her pillow and yielded to the impulse of her feelings and became so overcome with grief she could not utter another word.

Her mother, now being convinced that she could not comfort her, again left the room for a short time and when she returned found her Florence quiet, having fallen asleep. She watched over her with a mother's tender care, until overcome with fatigue herself, then rested her head on the pillow beside her darling and slept until morning.

When she aroused from her slumbers the next day, the dear Mama found the sun peeping through the bowers with all the loveliness and splendor that heart could wish. A gentle breeze that swept softly through the garden caught the fragrance of the many sweet flowers that had put forth in their beautiful clusters, and passed through the hall, filling every room with the odors of an April morning. She felt confident that the bracing atmosphere and the loveliness would have a tendency to invigorate Florence and do a great deal to restore her to her usually cheerful state of mind, but in this she was sadly disappointed, for when Florence awoke she complained of a very severe headache and much nervousness. She could not be prevailed on to eat anything and seemed to yield to a general despondency, although she was by nature usually of a cheerful temperament and always looked at the brightest side of life. Now that her fondest hopes had been crushed, her nerves became paralyzed. Sunk into a state of despair, she lost all interest in life, and seemed as if she did not care to live longer. During the day her head pained her so severely that medical advice was called in, and the physician, after investigating the case, pronounced it to be the result of excitement and only natural after the shock she had received. Leaving her such restoratives as he thought necessary, he bid her good morning, expressing the belief that all that was necessary was to follow his directions, and that a few days would be sufficient for her to be restored to health and beauty.

Florence began to regain her composure and the rose

began to return to her cheeks. For a few days it seemed that she would yet be well and happy, but ere long her color began to fade, and she was again attacked with violent pains in the head and shoulders. The physician had put his patient from his mind, when he was again called to her bedside to find that she was a victim of typhoid fever.

Florence continued to grow worse from day to day, until the once beautiful form and features looked almost like a corpse. Her weeping and murmuring had ceased and with calm and solemn resignation she rested quietly on her sick-bed and waited for the terrible disease to do its fatal work. None but those who have had some experience with typhoid fever can give any idea of the many long, wearying days and nights that were spent by her mother and friends around Florence, until the frail body could bear no more pain and sorrow, and yielded to the fatal Destroyer. Her spirit took its flight to brighter climes where wars, troubles and rivalry are known no more.

She died without ever knowing the whereabouts of Albert, whom she mourned as killed. Perhaps if she had known that instead of being killed he had fallen into the hands of the enemy and was then confined within the walls of a Northern prison, it would have been different with her; at least she would have been saved the torture of so much grief during her long illness. But she bore it all with calmness, and her last moments were passed in such a way as to leave the impression that she was willing to go, feeling that to depart and be with Christ was far better than a life of grief. Even the anxious solicitude and unremitting attention of a wonderfully devoted mother could not bind her to earth. The careful watching of friends could not delay her going, and it seemed as if the Destroyer desired to verify the old saying, "Death loves a shining mark."

Yes, Death with pinions spread wide
Bade the afflicted one to ecstasy arise,
And soar onward with joy and pride
To blissful mansions in the skies.

The frail flower withered and yielded to the decree of nature's God, who said, "Dust thou art, and to dust thou shalt return." After all the sacred rites had been bestowed by a grief stricken mother and friends, all that was mortal of the once beautiful, accomplished and Christian hearted Florence was laid beside departed friends, where she had delighted to linger in the beautiful Rose Hill Cemetery.[20]

XXI

Albert's Fate

AS WE HAVE TOLD THE READER that Albert was not killed as reported, we will now follow him through some of the scenes which he passed, until he learned of the death of the cherished idol of his heart.

On the day of the destructive battle in which he was thought to have been killed, Albert and other comrades were sent in front of the line of battle as skirmishers. During one of those terrific charges they were captured and hurried to the rear of the enemy's lines, where they were put under a guard and sent to the headquarters of General Meade, and thence to City Point* to receive transportation north.[21]

Albert now began to learn that the soldier who is never made a prisoner doesn't know what the extreme horrors of camp life can be. Although he found the veteran soldiers of the Federal army courteous and sympathetic toward the unfortunate Confederates who had fallen into their hands, there were many colored troops on duty around the prisons, and also many reserves and militia, who took a pride in

* General Grant's supply base and port for Northern destinations, at the Chesapeake Bay. Now Hopewell.

torturing and insulting the prisoners. Also, the Federal Government had adopted a line of policy that indicated a spirit of retaliation for atrocities at Andersonville; consequently Albert and his comrades were subjected to many things that were too humiliating and degrading to contemplate.

On the night of their arrival at City Point, they were driven into a stockade, and a large gate with a huge lock was turned on them, and there they were left to spend the night. The wind was blowing near a gale from the northeast, and the ground was covered almost completely over in crystals of ice. Here on this cold frozen ground without cover or shelter, the prisoners were compelled to lie and shiver with cold until relieved by the warmth of a morning sun. It was a great miracle that none perished with cold, being thinly clad, and entirely destitute of blankets, and denied the privilege of a spark of fire.

At early dawn the prisoners were up and walking to and fro over the crushing ice to keep from freezing. That night, the first he ever spent as a prisoner, will ever stand forth an isolated epoch in the chequered career of our hero.

Restrained of his liberty, guarded by former slaves and mortified by the shouts of foreign hirelings who were gloating with victory, the loud belching cannon pealing forth continual salutes in exultation over the day's victory, made every moment pass wearily to the prisoners, who could only think of the day's struggle as the entering wedge to the final downfall of the Confederate Capital. The thoughts of what might follow filled their minds with the keenest despair. The sound of the brass bands and the clatter of drums through the long hours of night brought a thrill of terror to the heart of every captive, as they well knew they were hearing the death knell of the Southern States.

The following day being the Sabbath, it served to add to

the comfort of the sun's rays as they glittered forth between the rifts and rendered the land and water more resplendent. During the day the citizen soldiery mixed and mingled with the prisoners, using every effort to induce them to desert the cause for which they had suffered so much, but these overtures were only treated with ridicule by the rebels.

At 2 o'clock in the afternoon Albert, with several hundred other prisoners, marched from the stockade to the wharf where they boarded the U. S. steamer Keyport, bound for a Northern prison. The whistle sounded the signal of departure, and the steamer glided pleasantly down the James, over the rippling waves, until darkness shut out from view every object except the beacon lights on shore. All night she moved quietly along until near morning the boom of the alarm bells could be heard, and an incessant signaling of whistles caused the prisoners to look from the deck to learn the cause of the signals. The numerous headlights that could be seen hung in the bow of other vessels informed them they had reached Fortress Monroe, where hundreds of vessels were congregated.

Here the compass was set, and the Keyport steered for a northern port. The wind was blowing from mid ocean, and the waves lashed the ship as she surged from billow to billow. The prisoners began to complain of seasickness, but as the sun began to peep up from the sparkling foam-crested waves, the wind began to calm sufficiently to make everything appear most lovely. On every side could be seen the white seagulls as they flapped along dipping the water, and then rising above the vessel to get a good view of the long streak of foam that followed behind the ship, churning up morsels of easy prey.

Albert went upon deck and gazed with silent awe at the mighty waters. Not a particle of land could be seen—nothing but the blue waters of the mighty deep, with here and there a vessel with sail spread gliding on toward the port.

Albert now turned his gaze toward Dixie, and wondered what had become of Florence. He knew that her heart would be almost broken unless she could learn of his whereabouts. He knew she would think him killed, as not one of the squad that he was with escaped to tell of their fate.

As he moved on he felt it very doubtful if they would ever meet again.

And while gazing toward Dixie, his mind was impressed with these familiar verses:

The land of my childhood is flitting,
Flitting from my view;
A gale in the sail is sitting,
Toil ye merry crew.

Here might my home be,
Upon the waters wide;
I could roam with a proud heart,
If she was by my side.

The wind come howling on the billow,
From the distant glee;
Storms a howling 'round my pillow,
Brings no fear for me.

Howl on ye dark waves
O'er the troubled tide;
I heed not your anger,
*For she is by my side.**

---

* "Maggie By My Side", *The Stonewall Songbook,* Richmond, 1864. Soldiers' field copies in Emory University Music Collection.

XXII

Prison

AFTER MANY MILES of the briney deep had been left behind, Albert turned his gaze from the direction of Dixie, and with sadness looked forward to catch a view of the port where he was to land amòngst strangers and enemies, who were employing every means at their command to crush the cause for which he struggled. As he well knew that they hated everything in the shape of a rebel, he could not expect anything but ill treatment at their hands. Consequently his heart grew faint and sick when he caught a glimpse of land, and beheld the stockade in which he was to be incarcerated. But his surprise can well be imagined when he found the veteran soldiers of the Federal army that were stationed at the prison not only disposed to be friendly, but ever ready to defend the honor of the Confederates, whom they considered their equals on the battle field. Being brave men themselves, they admired the gallantry of their enemies who were in their custody, but not so with the younger recruits and the colored troops. In many instances the latter were insulting, overbearing and tyrannical. Many of the white soldiers, also, who had never seen the battle field, were glad to have an excuse to kill and would do so with the least provocation.

When our hero was landed, he marched through the open gate of the stockade into the prison where about twenty-two thousand prisoners were confined, to await the termination of the war. When Albert looked around at the pale and haggard features of the inmates of this loathsome place, he felt that his chances for life were very slim. Turning his gaze towards a large tent near by, he caught sight of a ghost of horror in the shape of a huge pile of coffins that stood ready to receive the first ones that might fall victim to the many diseases that were prevalent in that detestable place.

Although the place was uncomfortable and the confinement so mortifying to the brave soldiers, yet many amusing incidents occurred that kept the prisoners from falling into despair. The jests that were got off by teasing the Negro guards would fill a volume if we were to attempt to give them in detail. But we will let the quaint sayings of Sergeant Jake and Corporal Dick rest with the past, and pass on to the day that will ever be remembered by every Confederate who was there confined in the Federal bastille.[22]

On that eventful day of which we speak, the sun had risen with brilliancy, and while its rays reflected on the sparkling waters of the deep blue sea, there was nothing transpiring to disturb the quiet prison camp or change the monotonous scenes, until the sound of the large guns on the gun boats aroused the Federal soldiers around the prisoners' camp, who caught the sound as if by magic. With the wildest excitement and enthusiasm they began to fire the cannon in the forts around the prison, followed by the sound of drums and playing bands amidst the deafening *huzzahs* of the Union soldiery.

This outburst of applause took the Confederates by surprise. They were at first perfectly astonished at the excitement in the Federal camps, but when the sentinels who were on top of the stockade began to cry out, "Peace, peace!" the rebels caught the inspiration and joined in the enthusiasm, and a yell such as had not been heard since Stonewall Jackson last rode down the lines went up from the prison camp. The word "peace," the sweetest word in the English language, fired the heart of every rebel prisoner and caused them all to join in the general rejoicing without ever thinking of the terms of the peace. They had but one thought—that the awful butchering had terminated, and the North and South would lay down their ams and return to loved ones at home. "Peace, peace," could be heard on every side, and that word conveyed all that was necessary to fill their hearts with joy. It meant liberty, home, comfort and plenty.

But their rejoicing was soon turned into weeping, and a sight greeted their eyes that caused the last gleam of hope to depart from their breasts. In the prison stood a lofty spire, from the top of which floated the Confederate flag, the pride of every true Southern brave. Thousands of lives had been sacrificed in defending this banner, for which they had struggled on many a hard fought field, and for which many a color bearer had yielded his life in preference to his colors—a flag now about to trail in the dust.

A sergeant with a guard entered the prison, and all eyes turned to them as they marched to the liberty pole. The rope was given a pull, the Confederate flag was furled and struck to the ground, and the United States flag ascended to the top of the spire, unfurled to the breeze, and floated triumphantly before the gaze of over-powered Confederates, who knew that the hauling down of their flag and the hoisting of the U.S. flag in its place was a signal that the Confederate armies had yielded to the armies of the invader, leaving their homes exposed to the mercy of an excited and exasperated enemy and the insults of emancipated slaves. The thought of subjugation, followed by emancipation, confiscation and probable extermination caused the stoutest heart to weep, and thus the rejoicing of thousands was turned into tears.

The Federal soldier who had hauled down the Confederate flag and hoisted the other in its stead turned to the prisoners, and pointing to the waving flag, said:

"Behold your protection. You are no longer prisoners of war, but citizens of the United States. You are brave men. We don't rejoice at the downfall of your armies because we desire to oppress you, but because we will in the future have the aid of your world renowned valor and indomitable energy in defending the government of the United States. The Union is ours, and the Union is yours. Let us be friends."

This brave Union soldier only spoke the sentiment of thousands of his comrades in arms, and if their sentiments could only have been carried out, this American republic, again reunited and cemented together with blood, would ere this have been the most prosperous nation on Earth. But alas, this has not been the case, notwithstanding that the true and brave of the Union army had an ardent desire to see chivalrous sons of the South restored to coequal rights. Yet there was a fanatical spirit that sprang up North and South among those who were non-combatants during the war that well nigh destroyed the republic and shattered the safe guard of constitutional liberty.[23]

Now after a decade has elapsed in wrangling, the passions of the war have subsided and every State of the Union is freed from military rule, and one of those brave Union soldiers raised to the pedestal of power,* who can say to the Confederate soldiers, "I acknowledge you had the right to fight for what you considered your rights, and I hope you will be as charitable towards me. There is no cause for us to be enemies, why should we not be friends?"

Yet on that day of the war's end, brave men wept like

* General Ulysses S. Grant, elected president for two terms, serving 1869-1877.

children; they felt that all that was dear to them had been crushed. When the confusion had somewhat subsided, the bulletin board kept by the Federals to inform the prisoners of transpiring events was hoisted on the inside of the prison near the entrance. On it was written in large letters a dispatch from General Grant, sent from Appomattox Court House, confirming the reported surrender of the army of Northern Virginia. Thus perished the last ray of hope for the Southern cause, and the men now in prison yielded to a state of despair. But the many kind tokens of friendship on the part of Federal soldiers, backed by promises of protection in the enjoyment of constitutional liberty and coequal rights inspired the rebels with renewed hopes, and caused them to yield more cheerfully to their fate.

Being assured that they would be allowed to return to their homes and rebuild their shattered fortunes unmolested, they acquiesced in the result of the war, and everything was arranged for their return home. They were daily expecting orders for their release, when one night they were again startled by the sound of cannon at intervals through the still hours of darkness. But this time the belching of cannon as the sound passed down the Potomac from one signal station to another and sent its echoes out across the Chesapeake bay to die away on the ocean, brought forth no applause, as it told of the saddest event yet known to the American people.

It is not known whether Southern prisoners ever actually displayed their flag at Point Lookout, but cases are documented of Northerners' flaunting theirs—at Andersonville (exhibited at New Hampshire Historical Society) and at Camp Oglethorpe in Macon (recorded in J. V. Hadley's *Seven Months a Prisoner*, N.Y., Scribner's, 1898, pp. 73-75).

XXIII

Release

WE HAVE SAID that the firing of cannon at half hour intervals told of the saddest event known to the American republic, and history will bear us out in the assertion. What deed is there more daring, what scene more appalling or what greater national calamity ever befell America, than the assassination of the President of the United States?

On the morning following the firing of the signal gun, the U.S. flags on the vessels were at half mast, and the flag on the spire over the prison floated at half mast. The early papers came out shrouded in mourning and the U.S. officials wore badges of mourning. All this was a mystery to the prisoners until the bulletin board was brought out on which was written the dispatch giving the details—the daring and blood thirsty John Wilkes Booth, jumping from the stage with a dagger in one hand and a pistol in the other, shouting *"Sic semper tyrannis!"* had sent a ball crashing through the brain of the President of the United States.

This tragedy proved that the suicidal war had no respect for person or position, but took its victims from the lowest hovel to the highest palace of the nation, and thus he who had reached the highest pinnacle of fame known to a republican government fell a victim to the passions of the war.

The assassination of the President paralyzed every branch of industry and locked the wheels of all business, thus preventing the release of prisoners and causing them to remain many days in great suspense. Days seemed like weeks and weeks like months to our hero. Not knowing what had become of home since the downfall of the Southern armies, he naturally felt very sad and often, sighing, sang:

Take me home to the place where I first saw the light,
To my sweet sunny South take me home;
Where the mocking bird sang me to rest every night,
Ah, why was I tempted to roam?
Take me home to the place where the loved ones sleep,
My poor mother is sleeping near by;
Amongst the graves of my loved ones I long to weep,
*And amongst them to rest when I die.**

After many days spent in anxiety and expectation of an early release, the prisoners finally settled down to make the best they could of their situation. Some went to work at making rings of buttons, others went to making fans of white pine plank, others making violins, others playing cards—keno, faro, and every other game that could be thought of to pass the time as cheerfully as possible.

The time finally rolled up for their departure, and after taking the oath of allegiance,[24] Albert boarded a vessel bound for Richmond, Virginia, and after a smooth voyage over a calm sea, touched at Fortress Monroe where the ex-Confederate President, Jeff Davis, was confined and surrounded by a large fleet of iron clad gunboats.

*Credited to Hewitt (Harwell, p. 37).

Here a short respite was taken and after a usual salutation the vessel glided smoothly up the James river to the fallen city. On this pleasant trip many points were passed that attracted attention: the famous Dutch Gap canal, the fortifications of Drewry's bluff and the remnant of iron clad vessels that had been sunk by the rebel thunder recalled to mind the fact that all the precious lives that had been sacrificed around that place had been all in vain. But before our hero could fully realize the awful solemnity of the surroundings, he caught sight of the charred walls of the once defiant, but now conquered and humiliated city of Richmond. One glance at the surroundings told that the torch had done its work. The Confederates, in leaving the city, preferring to see it succumb to the flames rather than become the property of the enemy, had fired it while leaving and added a double horror to the unfortunate citizens of the besieged capital.

After a night spent in this important place, Albert received transportation south, and was soon speeding on, past fortifications and bitter scenes, to the shattered city of Petersburg. After a few hours spent in this famous city, Albert bade farewell to the scenes of desolation, and with a buoyant hope of again seeing Florence and loved ones at home, boarded the train bound for Danville, where he was to take passage on the train that would bear him away to the once proud and prosperous State of Georgia.

When Albert took his last look at the noble old State of Virginia, he thought of her exhausted condition, her cities partially depopulated, homes destroyed, fields laid waste, fences burned and her once beautiful hills and valleys dotted over with the graves of the slain of every State of the Union and almost every nationality of the globe. He could not refrain from tears; thus his joys and sorrows were mixing and mingling together, each struggling for supremacy in his heart, but as the human heart always contains hope, and the imagination looks on the brightest side for the future, so it was with Albert. He thought of the noble sons of the down trodden State of Virginia and felt assured that with their ambition, enterprise and energy, they would be as true to their State in peace as in war, and if let alone would reclaim her fields, rebuild her cities, and restore her to her former magnificence and grandeur.

Thus it was that he pictured for her and her sister States of the fallen Confederacy a bright future and smooth voyage to prosperity. These thoughts, coupled with the inexpressible joy of an early greeting with Florence and loved ones at home, caused our hero to forget the sad events of the past, and he sped on with happy heart and joyous anticipations. Not having heard from home since he fell into the hands of the enemy, he was not aware of the fact that she with whom he had expected a happy greeting had been for months silent in the cold tomb. Thus we find in passing through life that it is not the best that we should know the future. If we did, many hours that we spend in joyous anticipations would be changed into long wearysome hours of repining, and weeping, and dread.

The sad news was to reach Albert when he least expected it. Arriving at Charlotte, North Carolina, he caught sight of an old comrade who was standing near the depot. This man had been too severely wounded to return home but was sufficiently convalescent to go on crutches to the car-shed. Albert jumped from the train and hastened to his acquaintance, and after the usual greeting his first query was, "What news from Georgia?"

"Bad news for you, I'm afraid," the friend replied in a sympathetic voice, and after a pause of a few moments, while Albert listened with breathless anxiety, his comrade informed him that Florence was dead.

XXIV

The Soldier's Return

THE TIDINGS of the death of Florence were to Albert like a thunder clap in a clear sky. He could not realize that his comrade was telling the truth until he was assured that there was not the least possible doubt of its being true.

When he once realized the fact that she who had given him her heart and hand was lying in the silent tomb, he almost wished he had been killed in battle. This was the greatest trial of his life. He had seen the great armies meet in conflict and the fury of battle sweep thousands of human beings into eternity; he had seen the pale moon shine over the fields each of victory and defeat and heard the most piteous cries of the dying and of children driven from home to face the pelting storm and beg for bread; cities in flames; helpless women fleeing for safety; brave armies crushed and forced to yield their arms to the power of superior numbers; and the stars and bars of the Confederacy trampled under foot—yet *her* sweet smiles, encouraging words and tender devotion to him had inspired him to bear all those trials with patience. But now learning that the heart which throbbed so fondly for him had been for three months silent in death, he cared not to live longer. He felt that all was lost.

Now that he had learned of the death of Florence, he was ready to believe any report that he might hear from home. He shuddered at the thought of returning home, as he contemplated the probable fate of those not heard from—perhaps father and brothers might have been killed and their remains left in distant States in the last struggles of the dying Confederacy. Perhaps home had been left, like many others, a heap of smoking embers, and mother and sisters driven out into the world to beg shelter of more fortunate neighbors. With such thoughts weighing on his mind it was natural that he would feel great anxiety and uneasiness, but he pressed on with a heavy heart, still hoping there might be some mistake regarding Florence's death. As he traveled on towards home, he met the victorious troops of Sherman returning north. They pictured to him the sad condition of Georgia by telling him they had made a graveyard of the State, and burnt the women and children out of house and home.

After many days of fatiguing travel, Albert reached Covington, Georgia, by train but had to walk the rest of the way, a distance of about thirty-five miles, only to find that his home stood in the track of Sherman's desolation, and that the reported death of Florence was really true. Dear reader, can you imagine what were the feelings of this careworn soldier, who but a tender youth of sixteen had entered the army with his heart all aglow with anticipations of a successful termination of the war? But after the years had elapsed, he had seen all his bright hopes vanish and the once happy scenes of his childhood made one vast expanding scene of desolation. What mind can portray a picture more sad than the one that presented itself to him as he neared his home, the many happy memories of childhood coming in contact with the sad events of the cruel and unhappy war!

Each sad scene presented itself, as his thought ran back a

few years to the time when the great nation was called to arms, when in the wild enthusiasm of organizing the military in every town, city or village in the land could be heard the sound of the fife and drum calling men to arms to slay their own countrymen. . . .

He sees them part from those they love. Some are walking for the last time in quiet woody places with the maids they adore. He hears the whisperings and the sweet vows of eternal love as they lingeringly part forever. Others are bending over cradles, kissing babies that are asleep. Some are receiving the blessings of old men. Some are parting who hold one another and press them to their hearts again and again and say nothing; and some, endeavoring with brave words spoken in the old tones to drive from their hearts the awful fear. He sees them part. He sees the wife standing at the door, with the babe in her arms—standing in the sunlight sobbing; at the turn of the road a hand waves. He is gone, and forever.

He has seen them as they marched proudly away under the flaunting flags, keeping time with the wild, grand music of war—marching down the streets of the great cities, through the towns and across the country, down to the fields of glory to do and to die.

He was by their side on the gory fields, in the hospitals of pain, on the weary marches. He was with them in ravines running with blood, in the furrows of old fields, wild with thirst, the life ebbing away among the withered leaves. He had seen them pierced by balls and torn with shells in the trenches and in the whirlwind of the charge, where men become iron with nerves of steel. He was with them in the prison of hatred and famine; but human speech can never tell what they endured.

He had seen those that had donned the gray fall facing those that had donned the blue; had seen the blue and the gray lying side by side in death. He had seen the blood of the blue and gray mix together on the field; had heard the midnight groans of friend and foe as they went together through the valley of death. He had seen thousands of men crowded together under the burning rays of a Southern clime, to sicken and die of disease and the tortures of prison life, and equally thousands of Southern men crowded together to be tortured by the severities of a Northern climate while guarded by former slaves. He had seen his fellow men left to decay and their bones bleach on the soil; had seen his countrymen tied to a stake and shot because they dared to leave the ranks a few hours to greet their wives and children; brave men cast into prison and bound with chains because they dared to speak their opinion. And now that the suicidal strife was over, he had learned that the beautiful, gentle and accomplished young lady who had pledged her all to him, had gone the way of all the earth.

Almost every family circle in the land had been broken—fathers and brothers from almost every Southern home had given the parting hand and never returned to the family again. Such heart rending thoughts, coupled with imagining the loss of property by the emancipation of slaves, the burning of cities, towns and villages, bridges, dwellings, barns and houses, fences, gardens and the driving off of horses, mules, cattle and everything that would feed man or beast—such thoughts drove him almost to despair. But with slow and feeble steps, Albert again reached home, in Butts county, where he received a hearty greeting, such a greeting as only a loving mother and sisters could bestow.

His mother was out in the yard when she saw a man, or boy, coming up the road. She shaded her eyes to see better but did not recognize him until he got to her. "Mother, don't you know me?" he said, and she cried out, "It's Albert!" He was so dirty and ragged and so emaciated she didn't know him until he spoke. She sent him to the river to wash, and burned his clothes, which were full of vermin. With no change of clothing, he had to wear his father's, until his mother could spin thread and weave cloth to make him some. There was great rejoicing in his home, as he was believed dead, since the others of the family had arrived home three months earlier.

Such a greeting inspired him with renewed hope and made him resolve to strike once more for his country, believing that what had been lost by the sword could be redeemed by forbearance, acquiescence and reason, aided by industry, economy and energy. Believing thus, he spent no time in repining but took position in the ranks of the struggling millions, resolved to bear his part in aiding all good men of all sections to work out the redemption of this great American republic, and at the same time build up and recuperate Georgia so that she would be the most brilliant star in the constellation of States that forms this, the greatest nation of Earth.

PART TWO

William, the Man

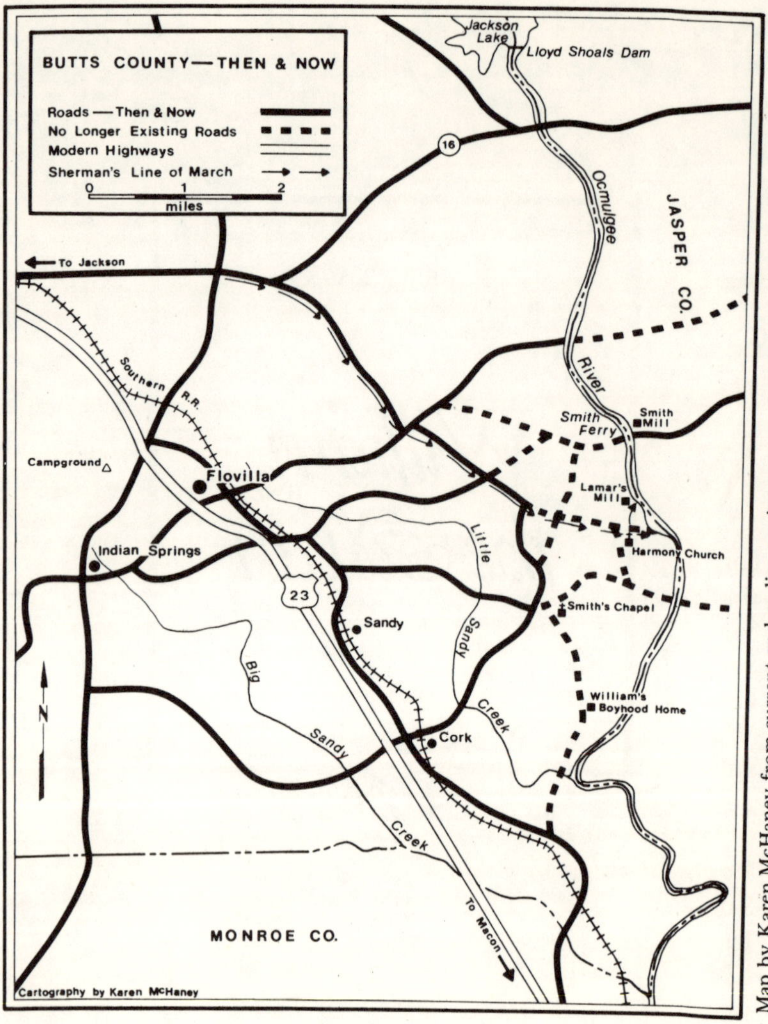

Map by Karen McHaney from current and earlier versions, courtesy of Marion Hemperley, State Surveyor General, and the Georgia Department of Transportation.

Butts County Then and Now.

William, The Man

A Biographical Sketch[25]

HARRIET S. KELLEY AND JEWELL G. SMITH

Beginnings

WILLIAM FERGUSON SMITH'S great-grandfather Robert Smith, son of Hughy, was born in Ireland in 1760, eventually settling in Butts County, Georgia in a community called Cork, in Dublin District near the Ocmulgee River and between its tributaries, Big and Little Sandy creeks. Robert fought in the Revolutionary War in South Carolina and was later given a land grant near the Creek Indian territories to the south. He married Ferguson Wilson, born on board a ship coming from Ireland in 1767, and named for its Captain Ferguson. Both Robert and Ferguson lived to be nearly 100 years old.

Robert's son Robert Wilson Smith married Virginia Jane Rowe, of Scottish descent, and their first of several sons, Samuel Ferguson Smith, was born December 14, 1819 in Fairfield District (Winnsboro, Chester County) South Carolina. The family came to Georgia when Sam was about nine years old.

The land where they arrived was lush and productive, and the spot on the river dividing Butts and Jasper Counties, described by William in "Cabin to College," was inspiring writers with the same charm a hundred years later. An Atlanta newspaper reporter told of the area in 1976 when he visited the Jasper location with a group investigating the place as a potential State Historical Site:

"While the swift, treacherous waters of the Ocmulgee River rush over rocks with a roar like that heard by 15th century Indians, birds sing in the pines, oaks, sweetgums and sourwoods on the shaded banks. The combination of sounds . . . beside the swirling stream is welcomed as a wilderness symphony in the tranquil setting where so much Georgia history has been made" (Salter).

A contemporary sketch reveals that Sam Smith, "his parents being poor, was compelled to begin labor in the field at the age of seven years, and his schooling was had at such times as could be spared from the farm. . . . On the 9th of January 1842 he married a daughter [Aney] of Mr. Parham Lindsey of Butts County" (Echols). Said William, later, "They embarked on the journey of life with no fortune except good health and sufficient energy to carve out of adverse circumstances and surroundings a handsome estate" (Obituary, 1889).

Sixteen children were born to the Sam Smiths; ten survived to maturity. William Ferguson, the second son, born September 16, 1845, was reared much like his father; he worked in the fields at an early age and attended school only rarely.

William makes fleeting reference to his childhood in various writings. In a letter to his father, Sam, dated March 20, 1886, he recalled:

> Tonight my mind flits back to childhood—when my innocent feet followed you home after the day's toil in the fields. I looked upon the canopy of heaven, and beheld with awe and admiration

the glittering stars, and asked you who made them. You said it was God.

I followed you in my childhood to the banks of the deep river, and gazed in wonder at the silent moving waters, with the leaves of autumn floating upon its bosom. I asked you who made the river. You said it was the work of God.

When you and that noble mother, who gave me life, endeavored to instruct me, you told me that God made us. When I asked why God made us, you said we were to serve him.

Do we fulfill the purpose for which we were created?

When I had grown to young manhood a nation's greed and sins involved us in a death struggle, and it was amid the scenes of blood and carnage, on the field of battle, I learned God could and would protect us, if we would ask Him. I also learned that He would answer the prayers of a Christian wife and mother, and protect sons who were too wicked to pray for themselves.

The Burden of My Soul is because we do not love and serve that God as we ought . . .

Here we can see something of the orgins of William's sentimentality, and the rapport he enjoyed with his parents in a relatively tranquil solitude before the family grew large and busy, and before times became complicated and difficult.

By the time of the Civil War, however, the simple and peaceful days were over. Sam Smith had become a prosperous farmer, owner of lands and mills and fine stock, yet he still considered himself "something of an old fogy" because he wore homemade clothes and raised at home the produce for his family, their servants, and his stock. This fierce pride in doing for one's self is a trait Sam passed on to his children, and they to theirs. He was ahead of his time in that he did not believe in planting cotton exclusively. "By his industry and economy he had accumulated considerable property but the war stripped him of almost everything" (Echols).

Young William, of course, did not know of this loss until he returned from the war in 1865. He describes his youthful zest to go to battle and his departure from home in his "Essay on the War" and "Confederate Women." He was the third of sixteen children, three of whom died in infancy and three of whom were born after the war began, so when he took his leave of home he was saying goodbye to a father and mother and eight little brothers and sisters. The oldest son, Wilson, was already at war, and the youngest, Bob, was only two years old.

Unfortunately none of William's letters survive from the war era, but it is evident from his story that he was homesick for the family he had left behind, and anxious for their welfare. Indeed, he had good reason to worry. His home was in the path of Sherman's destructive march through Georgia to the sea, which occurred at the same dreary time William was in the trenches around Petersburg. From there, we are told, "he would often look away to the southwest and imagine he could see the smoke of burning buildings," perhaps in the flame of winter sunsets (Chapter XVII).

Invasion

HIS DAUGHTER Jewell reminisced in 1977:

I remember they said Grandmother Smith, busy with her household duties, looked out the back door and saw two Federal soldiers riding horseback up to her front gate. Then to her surprise and horror she saw two of her little boys riding behind the soldiers. They had gone down the road "to see the Yankees." The soldiers had found the boys playing and asked them for whom their father voted in the last election, and they proudly answered, "Stephen A.

Douglass." It was thought that their reply was the reason Grandmother got by with so little property damage.

After conferring with Mrs. Smith, the officers took only what they needed for their immediate use. They asked for the family's guns, broke the stocks and returned them on the condition that they not be repaired until after the war (Ellis). Sam Smith was in the Georgia Militia and was in the fight near Atlanta July 22, 1864, and also at Griswoldville and was at Savannah when that city was surrendered (Echols).

One of the enterprises Sam Smith left behind when he went to fight locally was his mill, several miles upstream from his home, on the Jasper County side of the river. Smith's Mill was a grist mill that did a flourishing business. A large building served as a hotel or dormitory for people who came from as far as sixty miles away and waited, sometimes overnight, to have their corn ground fresh and to use the ferry, for which Smith made no charge. There was a blacksmith shop and a woolen mill and sawmill run by water power, a tanyard and a carpentry shop where coffins and carriages were made (Anderson). Today almost all traces of civilization—except modern picnickers and campers—have disappeared. Time, not battle, took the toll, for Smith's Mill was indeed spared by Sherman's men and prospered until around the turn of the century, when the building of the Jackson dam heralded the end of an era for the community. In the election of 1860 Smith had voted against secession; the invading army always made inquiry and tempered, somewhat, their treatment of those who were not actively "Secesh." Nevertheless, Sam and his family fully supported the Confederacy, and lost most of their personal assets in the war. William wrote of his father shortly after Sam's death in 1889:

He opposed the dissolution of the Union with all the power he could command, but when the lines were drawn he and his sons fought bravely and when the war closed he advocated reunion on the best terms we could get. He taught his children that honor and virtue were above price, and the brightest jewels one could possess in this life. (Obituary)

Another mill in William's family was the property of his maternal grandfather, Sam's father-in-law, Parham Lindsey. It was located at Seven Islands, not far downstream from Smith's Mill. This operation fared not so well in the wake of Federal forces.

Lindsey was born in South Carolina in 1789 and moved to Georgia where he married Polly Wise, settling in Jasper County across the river, to raise nine children, one of them William's mother Aney. Parham Lindsey was a delegate at the treaty of Indian Springs in 1825 and thereafter purchased land along the river where he built a grist mill at Seven Islands on one of the old Indian Trails, in 1828. Among his first customers were the native Creeks still in the vicinity (Lane).[26] Planters' Factory, built there in 1842, was a cotton mill owned by a company of well-to-do planters of Butts and adjoining counties.

As Williams says in his "Essay on the War," his grandfather Lindsey put everything he had into Confederate bonds, lost it all and died of a broken heart. Lindsey sold his land and holdings to Mr. C. A. Nutting in 1861 and moved to Spalding County where he died in 1863. At least he did not live to see its destruction by the Union Army the following year.

On the night of November 17, 1864, the Right Wing (15th & 17th Corps) of General Sherman's Army reached Jackson, Georgia. One division moved through Jackson and Flovilla to seize the ferry at Planters' Factory, nine miles southeast, and to secure both banks at that point for the passage of the troops next day (Scruggs). On the morning of November 18th the army began crossing the Ocmulgee River on pontoon bridges (Cox, p. 26; diagram Atlas, O. R., p. 106). The weather was cold and rainy, and the banks of the river so slippery, passage took longer than planned. Nearby, Parham Lindsey had built a nondenominational chapel, Harmony Church, on land he had donated for the purpose. General George Henry Thomas used the building as headquarters for several days while Federal soldiers completed their crossing and destruction at Planters' Factory. Ironically, *Smith's* chapel, whose mill was preserved, suffered the indignity of being used as a stable, and its pews taken for firewood to warm the troops (Lane).

General Sherman had ordered a disabling of all resources that could possibly offer any support to a rebel resistance, but the helpless victims of these losses saw a personal barbarism and vindictiveness in the acts of aggression. Such feelings, "inherited" from some of the survivors, are recorded by one of William's younger brothers, born after the war:

"The worst single act of vandalism committed in our county by Sherman's ruthless band of invaders was the burning of this cotton mill and setting the workers adrift without employment or means of support in the dark November of 1864. The building was built of timbers from the original pines of the nearby forest and the burning of it made a fire that could be seen for miles in every direction."[27]

More than 150 people had owed their living to the cotton mill, and many of them stood by and wept loudly as they witnessed the destruction of the machinery and loss of their livelihood. Even their livestock were confiscated and herded onto one of the largest islands in the river and shot. Thereafter the place was called Buzzard Island. That the workers managed to get through the winter and the next few

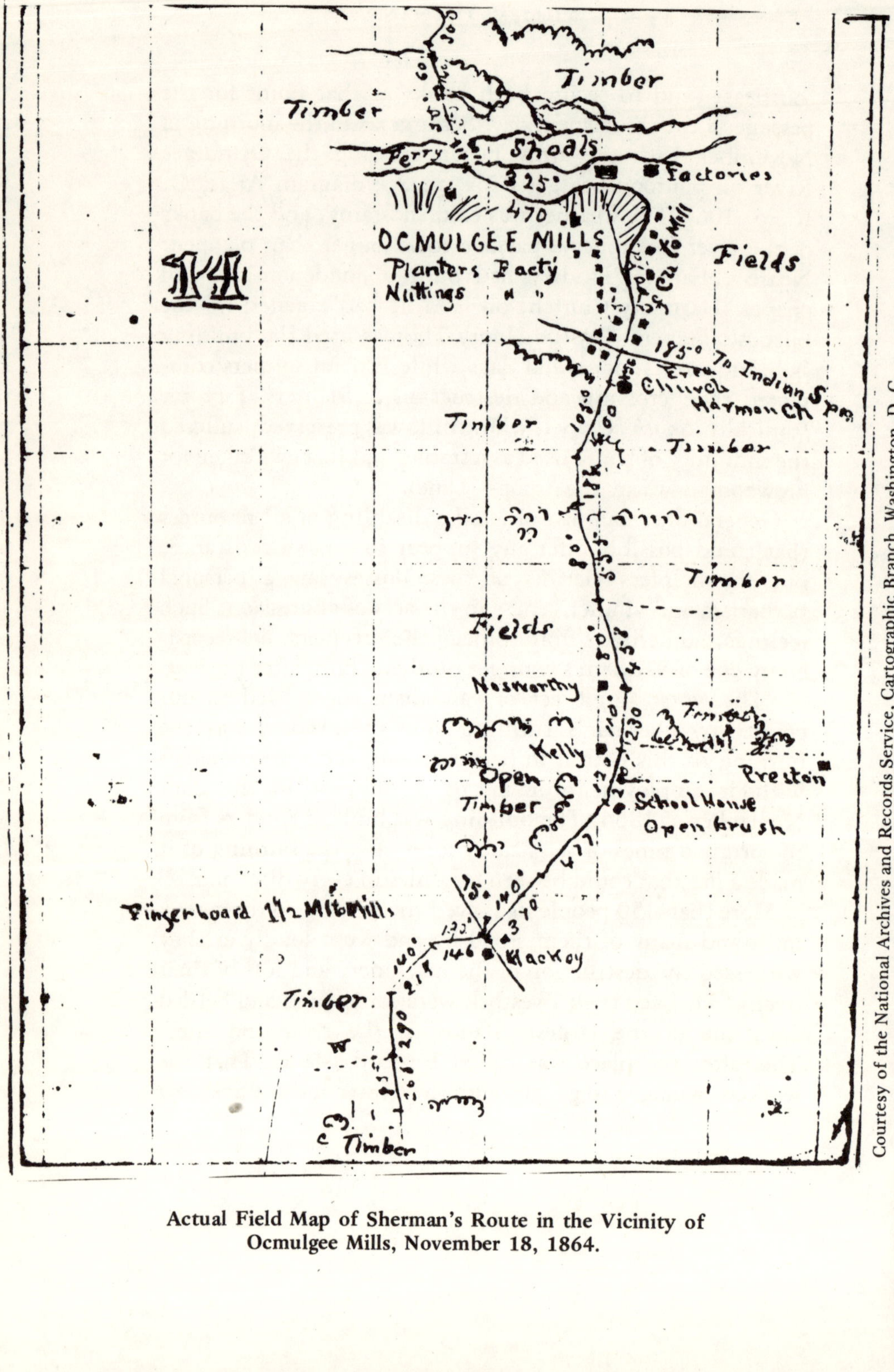

Courtesy of the National Archives and Records Service, Cartographic Branch, Washington, D. C.

Actual Field Map of Sherman's Route in the Vicinity of Ocmulgee Mills, November 18, 1864.

years is a miracle. The grist mill recovered somewhat, and was in operation again for a while as Ocmulgee and later Lamar's Mill, until the advent of electric power.

As the Union Army moved on in its march across Georgia, it made increasing havoc along the way, smashing crockery in homes and ripping open feather beds. A step-niece of William's, Clara Thompson Ellis (1886-1977) wrote: "I faintly remember hearing a tale about the soldiers' finding a cache of 'liquid corn' on the way and doubtless [it] made them more rowdy than otherwise they would have been." William's friends and family continued to be touched by the disaster. Jewell continues her recollections of the account of the march, after remarking that the Smiths got by with comparatively little property damage:

> When the soldiers came by my Grandmother Mitchell's home, however, they destroyed bales of cotton and burned the gin house. She begged them not to burn the [cotton] gin, the only way she had of making a living for herself and children, but they wouldn't listen. She was pregnant and as she watched the flames leap up, labor pains started. She sent an old slave to get her sister-in-law—walking, of course, two miles. The baby, my Uncle Dave, came before Aunt Beckie Beland could get there and my mother* who was only 11 or 12 years old had to help with the delivery. The soldiers stripped the smoke house, took the horses and everything else they could find. That was in Jones County not far from the river, about 4 miles from Juliette. Grandfather Mitchell was in service at the time. As well as I remember [hearing], the old servant had hidden a cow in a cane brake—she was not found and was Grandmother's salvation.

Thus when William, like Albert, "learned that his native State was to be subjected to the long train of horrors that

* "Patty" Mitchell, William's second wife, 1857-1948.

follow the course of an invading army he would often look away to the southwest and imagine he could see the smoke of the burning buildings in the track of the victorious . . . and the winter of '64 passed monotonously."

The Early After-Years

THE REST OF THE WAR moved rapidly to a close, from the time of William's capture and imprisonment, to his final release two months after Appomattox.

A grandson and namesake, William Ferguson Smith II of Proctor, Vermont, remembers his Aunt Willie's telling him that her father "did not want to talk about his trek home or his reaction to what he found upon his return. So Be It." At any rate, William had matured dramatically and perhaps painfully. He had rapidly become a man. Two years after the war, on Christmas Eve, he married Mary Talitha Preston (called "Clarissa" in her father's Will), a fifteen-year-old girl of his own neighborhood who was remarkably like his description of Florence. They settled in what is now the town of Flovilla, then "East End," which he helped to rename several years later (Jones, D.). William and "Tollie" had twelve children, one of whom, Nancy, died at age two and for whom William wrote an obituary that is one of his most moving testimonies. Mostly, though, it was a happy marriage and home life. In a letter to his wife from a business trip to Gainesville, Georgia in May of 1878,[28] William drew a row of little x's along the margin of the page—kisses for each of the then eight little ones, and counseled their mother to:

Kiss the children good night for me, and I will put one on the corner of this for you. Tell them all Papa says remember him in their prayers, and I will ask God to make them good children, and make them happy. It makes me feel very selfish to think of what I am enjoying while you are toiling for me and the little ones but all that can be done to make you happy by a tender devotion, and a pure unspotted heart will be bestowed upon you. I will close by giving a kiss below for each of the children. . . .

Your,
William.

Alice, the tenth child, and last family member to own the Flovilla home and live in it for any length of time, remembered vividly that their papa always brought them presents from his travels. Not only did he bring Alice at least two memorable dolls, but he also invented imaginative names and histories for them, introducing them to the little girls as if they were real ladies he had met and brought home for a visit. One, "Tiny," was a china child only an inch high. Another larger favorite was "Mary Anna Della Debonette," cloaked and hatted in velvet.

Meanwhile, William continued active in business, engaging in newspaper promotion and other interests for the development of his county. He, like Albert, had "resolved to bear his part in aiding all good men . . . to build up and recuperate Georgia . . ." and appears to have borne his part well. "While having been involved in several projects that were eminently successful, he never acquired any great wealth. Indeed after providing the simple comforts for a large and growing family what fortune he accumulated was quite modest" (Linch).

Neither was his father, Sam Smith, disheartened by the war and its losses, but with his wife went to work to more than restore his former position (Echols). In fact, it became a matter of grave concern to William in later years to see his father's apparent obsession with "laying up treasures on earth" (Letter, 1886). In 1876 Samuel Ferguson Smith was elected to the State Legislature. William, too, took an interest in politics; although he never ran for public office, he was chosen, that same year, to head the local militia unit and was known popularly as "Captain Smith" from then on. It must have been about this same time that *The Rival Lovers* was written, as the serial was published in 1877. He speaks of its being more than a decade after the war (Chapter V).

A love of language and writing came naturally to William; his mother is known to have written poetry.[29] Her prayers and lullabies, the songs of the slaves, as he has told us, and undoubtedly the name of familiar landmarks in the beautiful Indian tongue, all contributed to his appreciation for the rhythms of speech—Ocmulgee, Opothleoholo, Oboothlacoosta, Towaliga, Oakfuskee.*

His daughter Jewell says that he had a large vocabulary but was hesitant about speaking in public for fear he might mispronounce words he had read but never heard used, having only the equivalent of a third grade education. Yet notes for speeches have been found among his papers, and his surroundings, although unsophisticated, were by no means uncultured. There was a Mozart and a literary society in the town of Flovilla, and the climate and scenery and lifestyle attracted residents and visitors from as far away as New York and New England.

The Press and the Railroad

EVER ALERT TO happenings in the world beyond his own immediate environment, William learned, in the

* Original names of local streams and rivers.

early 1880's, that a certain company was planning to build a railroad from Atlanta through Newton, Jasper, and Jones counties to Macon.

> He obtained the interest of the officials by pointing out a shorter route along the western bank of the Ocmulgee River. This would develop many industries along the river and would give the railroad much more business. Upon replying the railroad company [Southern Railway] asked if he would be able to go out with their surveyors to point out the route. Going on horseback he helped survey the right-of-way. The first railroad entered Butts County on April 17, 1882. True to prediction, many mills and factories sprang up. (Settle)

The year 1887 was a dreadful one for William—as devastating as the war. Tollie died on March 2 at the age of only thirty-five, of complications from measles. Hattie, the second oldest daughter, then seventeen (1870-1940), was stricken with typhoid fever in June and did not get out of bed until Christmas. Others in the family were ill, and the youngest child was only nine months old.

William underwent a deep discouragement as revealed in some of his letters and articles of the next few years. Mary Talitha's obituary, preserved in her daughter Hattie's scrapbook, describes her as "meek and unpretending in her walk and conversation . . . an exemplary Christian, a good neighbor and a faithful friend. . . . The agony of her husband and children no language can portray. To them it was like striking the sun from the firmament, leaving the earth a dark and dreary void."

Two weeks later, William acknowledged the condolences of his fellow townspeople:

> When we are absorbed in the cares and anxieties of business life we are prone to indifference, and unmindful of our neighbors. . . . But when misfortunes overcome us, and our loved ones are torn

from our hearts [we] are made to rejoice when the sympathetic tear in every eye makes us all akin in feeling. We thank God for such friends and neighbors.

Misfortune did intensify William's sense of the spiritual dependencies of man, yet he stayed busy with his work and civic concerns, quickly becoming recognized as a leader among his fellow citizens. One of his keenest interests during these days continued to be the railway. This, as he described in a memoir on The Press, was one of his reasons for getting into the newspaper business. With characteristic humor he wrote:

Away back in the '70's the *Indian Springs Echo,* published by Harmon Edge, suspended. The press and type fell into the hands of Dr. Bryan, Sr., as junk. Dr. Bryan passed it on to me in a land trade as so much "to boot." Then I knew about as much about a printing outfiit as a hog does about a typewriter. Mr. Dumble was an old printer and he and I started the *Argus* and ran it awhile in the vacant residence of Dr. Bryan, now known as the Bryan House, run by Mrs. Keaton.

I built a brick room at the forks of the road at the Camp Ground and moved it there. The prime object I had in view in starting the *Argus* was to get a railroad thrugh Butts County. When the railroad was built I lost interest, and the paper was moved to Jackson and sold. (Jones, V.)

In an editorial some time later, William wrote: "Rapid transit is the most momentous question now before the traveling public." How modern that sounds! About 1888, a company was formed called the Flovilla and Indian Springs Railway, with Robert V. Smith, William F. Smith and George Elder as stock owners. The road was designed to transport passengers from the Southern main line in Flovilla to the resort of Indian Springs several miles away. The Dummy, as it was called, was extremely popular and profitable until the automobile forced it out of business in 1918. When it was sold for scrap during World War I, it brought more than the orginal cost of building the road (Johnson, p. 8).

After the little railroad was in operation, William, now "Captain Smith," was approached about establishing a religious campground near the route. Real estate was another of his many enterprises. During Christmas week, 1889, he was visited by representatives of two Holiness associations which held tent meetings at the invitation of pastors, mostly Methodist, in North and South Georgia. After much prayer, a location was selected about halfway between Flovilla and the Springs, between Macon and Atlanta, and between Columbus and Athens, thus almost in the center of the state and easily accessible from all parts of Georgia. Captain Smith was so impressed by the devoutness and earnestness of these men that he dedicated himself, with other friends, to securing the first ten acres of land for the camp and furnishing lumber and labor to build the first tabernacle on the grounds (Johnson p. 5).[30]

A related movement, that of attracting a denominational college to Butts County, failed because of a lack of support in raising funds, and this failure disappointed William greatly. Another disappointment was failure to complete a street railway system, or electric inter-urban line, even after rights-of-way and franchises had been secured. His discouragements were severe, and he wrote a great deal about them in the local press (Varner).

New Ventures

IN 1890, William was wed again—to young Miss Martha Elizabeth Mitchell, called "Patty," of Jones County. Four children were born, three of whom lived to be grown, and the family was whole once more. "He was a devoted husband and father," remembers Jewell, first child of this marriage.

Some of my happiest recollections are of his reading to us on hot summer Sunday afternoons, and of his autumn walks with us in the woods to look for wild haws and nuts. He was a great lover of nature, and in the spring as we explored the woods together, he taught us to know and love the things we found there. He would cut small limbs from a tree whose bark would slip easily, to make whistles for each of us. Papa was also a lover of music and he enjoyed playing a fife. We still own and cherish the fife he used while in service. He was an early riser and usually awakened the other members of the family with the singing of some old ballad or religious song, and it was not hard to guess his mood by the song he was singing.

The weekly press continued to play a prominent part in the history of Butts County, and journalism continued to occupy William, off and on, for the rest of his life. In summarizing this involvement, he wrote:

When the panic of 1893 came on it seemed to me that the money powers had the people by the throat and was determined to crush them. It was then I bought the press and outfit owned by the *Progress* and started the *Headlight* at Flovilla and joined the eighteen hundred Populist* papers in the United States in a desperate effort to better conditions.

In a few years all our demands were either made into law or put in the platforms of the two old parties. Then I lost interest in the printing business and again that outfit was sold and moved to Jackson. (Jones, V.)

---

* The People's Party, formed in 1891 to protect and unite Black and White farmers against moneyed private interests.

A proliferation of editors and papers occurred over a period of time until 1908, when the late Doyle Jones, Sr., took over the combined publications and began a tradition lasting until the present time. His son, the late Doyle Jones, Jr., wrote in 1976, "Probably these two men, Smith and Jones, two uncommon men with common names, did as much to shape the destiny of Butts County as any two citizens who ever shared the same common ground" (*Jackson Progress-Argus,* 1 July 1976).

One of William's greatest dreams did finally come true, in a spectacular way. In connection with the electric streetcar network he envisioned, William went in search of available water power. Meditating over his own Ocmulgee River, at Lloyd Shoals, the thought came to him, "Oh, what nature has done for mankind here and we stand and let the shoals murmur at our neglect!" (Varner). He bought land on both sides of the shoals but he, alone, could not afford enough, even with the help of interested friends who pooled resources to acquire the properties. Finally, with the aid of Mr. Jordan Massee of Macon, Northern capitalists became interested and advanced the necessary money (Walden). Thus the Ocmulgee or Lloyd Shoals Dam, the first large hydroelectric plant in Georgia, was begun. In March of 1909 the project was well under way, and was celebrated with a huge barbecue honoring all investors, who were brought south on a special train to witness construction.

"One of the interesting events of the day was the meeting of two promoters—one who has put large sums of money into the undertaking and the other years of study. Suave and affiable Mr. A. B. Leach of New York, and plain Captain W. F. Smith of Flovilla were presented to each other, and the pleasure each one felt in the introduction was evident." William had labored twenty-five years for this end (Varner).

The Final Days

THE OCMULGEE PLANT went into operation just a year before his death, but William did not live to see the realization of his greatest desire—power turned on in simple country homes as it is today. It was thought that failure to see all his fondest ambitions fulfilled for his countrymen may have hastened his decline and death (Obituary 1912). In January 1910 he underwent treatment for ill health in McDonough, Georgia, and undoubtedly anticipating his end, wrote the following letter to one of his daughters:

Dear Laura,

This is for all my loved ones and friends. There is something I would tell you but my emotional nature forbids. Some of these nights I may pass away like the melting of a snowflake. The sins of my early life have been blotted out and I have the assurance they will not live after me. In my later life I have done the best I could with my environment. . . .

I care nothing for death if it were not for the bonds of affection, and the effect it would have on my loved ones and others. It may be God's good purpose to spare me more years. If so, I shall try to carry a ray of sunshine wherever I go. Under all circumstances, you all must hold on to the "golden Rule." It may seem at times as if it will break or fail; but if you will hold on, the storms of adversity cannot blow you away from it. . . .

He lived just over two years longer and continued to leave and send messages of hope and encouragement until the last—an article describing an experience of Angels, and of a rafting trip down the Chattahoochee river into Florida, a diatribe against the lawlessness he saw developing in his county, his summary of the history of the press (Varner). Another interesting document of his later years is a history of the U.S. from 1860 to 1960, titled, "The Death of the

American Republic," a lively projection full of wit, compassion and sometimes fiery indignation. William felt that "government by the people" began to decline when common Americans began to be afraid to elect members of their own class to represent their interests in Washington, choosing instead lawyers, and "the best orators." Among his papers is a letter from the editors of *Men of Mark in Georgia,* inviting him to submit biographical data for inclusion in that directory. Whether from illness, oversight, or typical modesty, he never replied.

A resident of the county, Miss Jo Varner, whose home was the famous McIntosh House at Indian Springs, made a scrapbook for Captain Smith during his last illness—a large catalog of newspaper clippings summarizing his distinguished yet unpretentious career. Her handiwork is a valuable record of his history.[31]

William Ferguson Smith died at his home in Flovilla on March 16, 1912, and was buried beside Mary Talitha in the Sandy Creek cemetery, between Flovilla and his ancestral community of Cork. This land, where Robert, Robert-Wilson, and Sam Smith all had lived and died was the most thickly settled and most prosperous part of Butts County until the Civil War and for some years after. The Ocmulgee River still flows steadily on, joining the Oconee to form the Altamaha on its way to the sea. But with the building of the railway in 1881, there came a change of business sites from the fertile and heavily timbered river lands, to several miles further west, and with this movement a shift of population (Smith, K.). The old farm house William left as a boy stands today in ruins, on land leased by a large paper company and inaccessible to approach. The millrace, a few stone wheels and metal rods are all that is left of Planters' Factory. The thriving roads of the early setting are overgrown to forest, almost as primitive as in William's earliest childhood. Yet his efforts and vision were largely responsible for the developments which helped bring his county into the twentieth century in a tangible way. William's role has not been forgotten—the Bicentennial edition of the county paper he helped to start carried many references to his pioneer groundwork; and his descendants—teachers and journalists, engineers and businessmen, doctors and lawyers and statesmen—have spread across the nation, but those who remember him personally are few.

JEWELL, his last remaining daughter, offers a belated tribute in summary, perhaps the gentlest memoir of all:

Papa was a devoted husband and father. He was deeply spiritual, converted on the battlefield, and his faith was long-enduring. He helped organize and build the Baptist Church in our little town of Flovilla, and was a deacon in that church as long as he lived. How well I remember walking with him to Sunday School, where he was the superintendent for more years than I can remember.

My father loved his country, state, and county. For more than a generation he was prominently identified with every movement for the advancement of Butts County. The best years of his life were spent working enthusiastically for its development. He spent liberally of his time and resources in planning and building for future growth.

He foresaw the possibilities of water power development on the Ocmulgee River, and worked for this until he lived to see the water harnessed and supplying electric energy to cities and factories throughout Middle Georgia. When the authorities wanted to name the project for him, he modestly declined the honor, saying the works belonged to all the people. It is now popularly known as Jackson Lake and Dam.

He played an important part in getting the Southern Railway built through Butts County when another route had been surveyed. He rode on horseback and secured rights-of-way from Atlanta to Macon.

My father was a pioneer newspaperman in the county. When he first started his paper at Indian Springs in 1875 he set type by the light of a little brass lamp, with the Washington hand press then in vogue. The paper was the *Middle Georgia Argus.* It changed names several times and moved to Jackson. Today it is the *Jackson Progess-Argus.*

His own education having been interrupted by the War Between the States, he was ever mindful of what he had missed and anxious to see that others were given a better chance. He worked untiringly to build the best possible school in his home town.* Music, art, and "elocution" were among the opportunities offered. Consequently many pupils from surrounding counties came there as boarding pupils.

He saw to it that not only his own children had the opportunity for a higher education, but he also contributed to others whatever he was able. For example, he lent encouragement as well as tuition to his sister-in-law, Amanda Jane Mitchell, to attend medical school in middle life, when no one else believed she could or should. In 1909, at the age of forty-six, she became one of the first women physicians in Georgia.

He was a gentle, kind, and sympathetic man but spirited and vigorous in defense of his convictions. He was a staunch advocate of law and order, and he worked always for temperance and good government.

Although he had volunteered his services in the Confederacy and had written *The Rival Lovers,* a story of the war-torn

* Established September 1, 1884, as Indian Spring High School at "East End," later Flovilla (Varner).

years, in later life he was reluctant to talk about his experiences and was never very expansive on the subject. He said, "It is over now, and we are one nation, a united nation and we must make it the best nation possible by being the very best citizen we know how to be."

Once, his youngest son asked him if he had to serve again in the armed forces, wouldn't he prefer to serve in the cavalry rather than the infantry. My father replied, "I wouldn't prefer either." When the question was pressed, he said rather sadly, "Dave, I would prefer to know that there would never be another war, and to know that you or any other young boy would never have to take up arms against an enemy."

After seven months of service in the battalion of underage boys in Macon, Georgia, he was used as a replacement for the war-thinned ranks of the Army of Northern Virginia. He was assigned to A. P. Hill's Corps, Wilcox Division, Thomas Brigade, 45th Georgia Regiment, Company I, where his older brother Wilson was already serving.

His adventures were those of Albert in *The Rival Lovers,* so far as we know. With all the hardships he endured, he had no malice in his heart and longed to see a united nation, united in spirit and brotherly love as well as in name.

PART THREE

Other Writings of WFS

I

From Cabin to College
From the Plow to the Presidency

(An Unpublished Manuscript)

ON THE LINE of Sherman's March from Atlanta to the Sea, at the point where he put in his pontoon bridges and crossed the Ocmulgee river is one of the most picturesque scenes in the South. In the days long ago it was known as Seven Islands, later Planters' Factory, then still later, Ocmulgee Mills, now Lamar's Mill.

In a pioneer cabin that stood on one of the romantic hills that overlooked the Ocmulgee river, I was born in the year 1845. Here, in Butts county, Georgia, I imbibed the Spirit of freedom and the love of country from the enchanting woodland scenes by day, and the lullaby of the roaring water by night. And now memory carries me back to the roar of the river, the bending willows, the honey suckle, and the dogwood bloom and sweet-shrub and the fragrance of the forest.

Following the plow in my father's* low grounds along the

---

* Samuel Ferguson Smith, 1819-1889.

banks of the river, I learned to love and sympathize with the toilers of the land; and keeping step in the furrow, to the songs of the Slaves, I learned to love its melody.

I attended school with the boys and girls whose brothers and sisters and parents worked in the cotton mill, joined them in ball games, etc. I also worked in the fields with the black slaves and joined them in fishing and hunting on our holidays.

The earliest of my childhood recollections was waking before dawn to hear above the roar of the rushing waters of the river the sound of the bugle calling the black slaves into the frosty low lands to pick the cotton, and the sound of the bell calling the white slaves into the mill to handle the frosty looms and spindles in manufacturing the cotton.

Seventeen years on the farm, with two or three months of schooling in the country school house, after "laying-bye"* time each year, brought us up to the war. A slight wound received in the battle of the Wilderness, Virginia, sent me to the college in Lynchburg (the same having been converted into a hospital) where I spent a few days, this making the sum total of my collegiate course.† Therefore I ask that a generous public pass over the grammatical errors without criticism.

The Federal Soldiers in their policy of destroying the resources of the South burned the cotton mill [near my home], but left the grist mill standing in response to the appeals of the women operatives of the cotton mill. After the war the abandoned cottages fell into decay, the grist mill

* The period in late summer after the final cultivation of the crop when the planting is put to rest until the time of the harvest.

† Lynchburg College was abandoned in 1861 when most of the faculty and students joined the Confederate Army. It was later reopened and is in operation today.

came to ruin, and the mawkish building now stands as a lame sentinel guarding the history of a dead past.

Now, under the headline "From the Plow to the Presidency" we do not mean the Presidency of the U. S. but the Presidency of a railroad.* Forty years service in the various positions of farm labour, manager of farm laborers; private soldier in camp, on the field, in the hospital, in prison; through Reconstruction in the South, a manager of freed men on the farm, a manager of freed men as a railroad contractor, and as a builder of a railroad and as president of a railroad, my observation brings up in my mind the query: "Is this a dying Republic?"

The answer will be given by the farmers and laborers of America. Let them act their part as patriots and the Republic will be saved. Let them be indifferent to their liberties or controlled by prejudice, and the Republic dies. . . .

Can we—will we—perpetuate this Republic for the benefit of the children of both races? Or will we allow race prejudice and sectional hatred to rob us of reason, smother our patriotism, and engage us in factional strife, while our great Republic goes down under the threatening grasp of financial despotism?

I present these questions for the thoughtful, prayerful consideration of the great middle class of the American people to consider, with the hope, the prayerful desire, and sincere belief, that the great responsive heart will answer in the affirmative.

To those who wore the blue and the gray; their sons and daughters, and to my mother†, who taught me of the fatherhood of God and the brotherhood of man, this work is dedicated.

---

* Flovilla and Indian Springs Railroad.
† Aney Lindsey Smith, 1823-1894.

II

An Essay on the War

(An Unpublished Manuscript)

THE GREAT NATIONAL DEMOCRATIC convention had met in Charleston and the Northern, or anti Slavery wing had nominated Stephen A. Douglass of Illinois. The Southern or Slavery wing had walked out of the convention and called another convention to meet in Baltimore at a later date.

The Baltimore convention met and nominated John C. Breckenridge of Kentucky, the Whigs nominated Bell of Tennessee and the Abolition party nominated Abraham Lincoln of Illinois, and the four cornered fight was on.

In fact those who can remember those stirring and exciting days bear in mind that the row in the Charleston convention resulting in the severing in twain of the Democratic party was really the beginning of the civil war, as this split in the Democratic party made it possible for the Abolition party (as the Republican party was then called) to elect a President, and there was really no peace between the sections after that was made possible, until the Slavery question was fought to a frazzle at Appomattox.

The fight between the two factions of the Democrats became so bitter that the "Know Nothings" as the Whigs were called and the Abolitionists seemed to be almost forgotten in the political strife until they all awakened one fine morning to find that Lincoln was elected.

After John Brown made his raid on Harper's Ferry in an attempt to get the "Negros to Rise," the word Abolitionist was the most despisable word known in the South.

If a person wanted to insult another there was no better way than to call one an Abolitionist, and no surer way to get up a fight. So you can imagine what a wave of indignation swept over the South when it was known that Lincoln was elected. This storm of indignation ripened into a determination to secede from the Union by the "fire eaters," as the extreme element were called.

Oh! Those exciting times!

Everywhere it was Secession and Union, and those discussions grew more heated and feeling ran high all over the South until State by State fell into line to form the Confederacy. After the firing on Sumter there was no more discussion of Union or Secession, and except in the border States there was no more division of sentiment. In every Seceded State every one knew it was to be a life and death struggle for self defense.

There began organizing of the Militia companies all over the South and the fife and drum was heard early and late. I shall never forget the day when Mr. Park Fears, a middle aged neighbor, came over the hill to our school house, keeping step to the rat-tat-ter-tat of a kettle drum which he carried, and calling out, "Fall in, boys! Fall in!"

We had no telegraph or telephone lines then and only a

twice a week mail. News was carried by the word of mouth, and of course many wild rumors and exaggerated reports were made of transpiring events.

The news that came to us, outside of the semi weekly mail, came by stage line from Forsyth to Indian Spring. The writer was a boy too young for enlistment in the companies then organizing and did not enter the service until two years later, after all the fun and frolic of camp life had been knocked out. Indian Springs being head quarters for news, every one who went to town came back with some startling news.

I can remember how I stood in open mouth wonder and listened to my uncle Johnathon [Lindsey] tell of the great fortifications they were building around Charleston. He had seen a man at Indian Springs who had been there, and told of the wonderful guns &c. Said the boys in their daily practice would take empty barrels in a skiff out 3 miles to sea and put them afloat and the gunners in the batteries would knock the head out nearly every shot with their cannon. Said the combined navies of the world couldn't take Charleston. Poor Uncle Johnathon; he believed all this, and died in camp, and was buried in Charleston and never lived to see Sherman's army march into and through the city from the rear, almost without the firing of a gun.

At Indian Springs the Butts Volunteers, the first from Butts county, were being drilled. Dennis Long, a young Irishman, beat the bass drum, the largest one it seemed to me I ever saw. We lived in the valley of the Ocmulgee river 6 miles away and could hear distinctly, morning and afternoon, the sounds of the martial music which thus kindled into all the boys around about a desire to be marching with the Volunteers.

Our older brother had an unusually large foot for a sixteen year old boy and when he expressed a desire to join, "Uncle

Arch," one of our colored men said, "Yes, and you'll git shot in the foot first round."

Later, when brother had joined a company and gone to Virginia, "Uncle Arch," who had a wife with Mr. Hugh Heard, who owned the farm where Flovilla now stands,* had gone, as was the custom among the slaves, to spend Saturday night and Sunday at his wife's house, and came in Monday morning with startling news.

The stage had come in with letters and papers telling of the seven days' battles around Richmond. Seeing my mother he said, "Lordy Madam! They have been fightin' all the week, and jes' like I told, that boy's shot through the foot, and a whole passle on 'em killed."†

About the time of the beginning of the excitement leading up to the war, a young man took up residence in our community, coming from Columbus, Georgia, where he had belonged to a military company. This young man, Albert Burton, brought with him some part of his uniform, and when dressed in his "round-about jacket" was the envy of all the boys in the community; they would gather around him to hear him explain. The strap sewed in where the sleeves were sewed to the coat, and the other end carried up and looped over a button on the collar, was put there to protect the coat from the wear of the gun carried on the shoulder. The one on the left shoulder would keep the strap of the haversack, in which rations were carried, and the strap of the cartridge box from slipping off the left shoulder, when it was buttoned down over the straps. The straps of the knapsack in which extra clothes were carried on the back were to be held in place by passing under the shoulder strap

---

* Flovilla was first called East End, or East Indian Springs, later Heard's Station; named Flovilla in 1887 (*Jackson Progress-Argus,* I July 1976)

† At Frazier's Farm, Virginia, 30 June 1862.

on both shoulders. The straps on the side of the coat at the waist held the belt in place on which the bayonet and cap box were carried. And many other details he could give to the boys who had never seen a soldier in uniform.

Many interesting things in regard to the details of a battle he could also rehearse to the boys, though he had never been in battle but got it from those soldiers who had. He said that sometimes when they fought with Indians they would either get tired of shooting their guns or get short on ammunition then would set their guns aside and pick up the arrows the Indians had shot at them and pitch them back at the Indians. These and other rehearsals had fired the heart of many a hearer with a desire to become a soldier.

My Grand-Father [Parham] Lindsey, who had represented Butts county in the Legislature* was a staunch life long Democrat and a consistent Hard Shell Baptist, and went with the majority to become an ardent Secessionist. So sure of success of the Southern cause, he actually sold his fine plantation on the Ocmulgee river (now owned by Walter Lamar) and put the money into Confederate bonds and lost every dollar of it.

Poor Grand-Father lived to see his mistake and I always believed he died with a broken heart. His grand-son he had raised went off with the Butts Volunteers to Yorktown, Virginia and died without ever firing a gun in battle. Another grand-son went to Savannah with the 30th Georgia Regiment and died in the same way. Other near and dear relatives were shot to pieces and some killed, and before his death [in 1863] he said he would give everything he possessed in the world if he could just stop the war and put us back where we started.

In Macon, Georgia, a Battalion of boys under age was

*State Senator 1834, 1840; House of Representatives 1841.

being organized to guard the Government works, guard prisoners and be ready for the defense of the State. For service in this Battalion Albert Burton and three of four other boys, including this writer, volunteered from Butts county.

III

The Execution of Roe Dickson

This portion of the story was found in three parts, separate from the main narrative and several years earlier. The first part was in manuscript, penciled on the reverse side of pages from an old typesetters' catalog. The sheets were not numbered and the margins so badly deteriorated that part of the text had to be imagined and reconstructed. The second and third sections were published in the Butts County Argus *in 1880 under a heading of "Chapter IX: A Barbarous Scene" so we believe they were intended to fit into the sequence as a part of* The Rival Lovers, *though very much of a digression. These pages were introduced with the heading: "By request of some friends we publish this chapter of 'A Southern Story of the Late War' by W. F. Smith, before printing the story in book form. As there still survives in this county several participants in the scene portrayed in this chapter, it will no doubt interest them. Entered according to act of Congress in the year 1880 by W. F. Smith, in the office of the Librarian of Congress at Washington."*

BEFORE FOLLOWING the Army on its march from Orange Court House, the writer will devote a few pages to the details of a military execution in which a brave soldier was sacrificed that army discipline might be preserved.

Perhaps there are many survivors of the war who have witnessed the execution at the stake of some of their comrades in arms, and we dare say that no more heart rending and blood curdling scenes ever met the gaze of any one. As I do not wish to play the historian, who paints only the glories of war, hence I cannot refrain from giving a sketch of the horrible scene at Orange Court House, Virginia, by the sentence and execution of Roe Dickson, a member of the 14th Georgia Regiment, whose life was sacrificed at the stake by a military court on a charge of "desertion in battle."

Young Dickson had borne the name of good soldier through all the bloody struggles of the war up to the time of the historic battle of Gettiesburg where he was found to be absent when his command prepared to join battle for the onslaught against an impregnable position. He had entered the service at his country's first call for troops, and was a member of the company organized and carried into service by Captain Folsom who afterwards became colonel of the Regiment and remained in command of it until he was killed in the Wilderness on May the 6th, 1864.[32]

The 14th Georgia Regiment was one of the bravest ever sent to the field, and Dickson stood shoulder to shoulder with his brave comrades on many a hard fought field. No matter how dear the cost, nor how great the sacrifice of precious lives, the 14th Georgia knew nothing but success from the time they joined the stubborn resistance to McClellan's Peninsular Campaign, until the turning point at Gettiesburg.

He stood with his Regiment at Fair Oaks, and served with distinction. He went with his comrades in the historic charges of the "Seven days' fight around Richmond," where the foe was hurled reeling, dismayed and defeated, and driven back to the distant shores of Maryland, strewing their pathway with blood as the Confederates swept them on towards Washington.

Yes, he stood by his colors while his Regiment with the Confederate army was driving that overwhelming opponent step by step from the soil of Virginia, and finally penetrated the enemy's country, vaulting over prostrate and conquered armies to plant the Confederate flag beyond the Potomac on the heights of Maryland.

From the second battle of Manassas to the embattled heights around Harper's Ferry with their hundreds of frowning cannon belching hurricanes of shot and shell, there offered no obstruction to the victorious A. N. V. as the thunder of Sharpsburg pealed forth with deafening echoes through the mountain passes and over hill and plain, carrying terror to the occupants of this Federal Capital, and notifying them of the approach of the bristling steel and stream of fire of the Rebel army.

The Confederate army after driving them into their strongholds, retired to "Winter quarters" on the soil of Virginia, and was attacked during the winter at Fredericksburg, and with the strength of giants, hurled the enemy back across the river and then again at Chancellorsville, when the enemy was again so badly beaten as to again seek safety in retreat.

Up to this time the Confederate army knew nothing but victory. Yes, victory after victory had been gained over superior numbers, until the soldiers had become in their own estimation invincible. They had reached that point of enthusiasm that has always, in all ages of the world, culminated in disaster, that feeling of confidence that inspired the belief that strict discipline is not essential to the further defeat of an opposing army that had been driven from many fields torn with shot and shell, and sent retreating towards the strongholds of their own Capital. Just such a feeling of confidence as this pervaded the Confederate army when they began the pursuit of the Federals which resulted in the disaster at Gettiesburg. Is it any wonder that each private soldier would consider himself almost a General, when they had been so victorious?

The march was through a country that had more than once been laid waste by an invading army, and as the commanders were desirous of pushing the enemy as rapidly as possible to prevent them from recruiting their retreating columns, this necessitated a very rapid march, causing many to fall, footsore, by the wayside from exhaustion and hunger, and many other diseases, such as dysentery, etc., caused from exposure and subsisting for many days on such things as roasting-ears and green apples and such other things as could be gathered up by the foraging parties. During this ever memorable march the battle scarred Confederates did not consider it a breach of discipline to fall by the wayside for a few hours' rest, or leave ranks for a short distance in search of something to fill "canteen or haversack," for they would, unless exhausted, soon return to their proper place in ranks, but many fell by the way who could never again recover the lost ground, and many who fell victim to disease and exhaustion would call on the surgeons of the army and get a certificate of disability, and if they could not get conveyance on an ambulance would have to seek shelter for a few days with some citizen by the line of march. Others with slow and feeble step retired towards Richmond and the cities of Virginia with the hope of finding rest amongst those whom they had so nobly defended; others sought shelter with the hospitable settlers in and around the mountains. Among the crowd that fell by the wayside was Roe Dickson, the subject of this sketch.

He carried a certificate in his pocket, and lodged with a farmer in the mountains of Virginia. Whether he would have returned to his duty after recuperating his health, or whether he intended to prove traitor to the cause for which he had so nobly fought, no one but the Great God, who knows all the emotions of our hearts, will ever know—we can only take his word for it and judge by his past actions whether he acted in bad faith or not; that he was a deserter in the true sense of the word, we will never believe. The surgeon whose name was signed to the certificate claimed that it was a forgery, and hence the charge of desertion for which Roe Dickson atoned with his heart's warm blood.

That the carelessness of the Confederate soldiers to keep "closed up" in ranks on the march when they could not feel the need of it, and falling out from exhaustion or illness, was the prime cause of the defeat at Gettiesburg cannot be disputed. The Confederate army grew weaker every step by the loss of its soldiers, while the Federal army they were driving before them was like the rolling of a snowball—gathering up strength at every step as it fell back upon its own resources and its own territory, gathering strength every hour until it reached Gettiesburg. There, reinforced by the militia of Pennsylvania, and all the available troops around Washington, it seemed that nothing was lacking to enable the Federals to defy the balance of the world.

To those insurmountable heights all eyes of the Nation were turned; the life of the Nation was in jeopardy and the public pulse had risen to a fevered heat; the soil of the great State of Pennsylvania resounded to the tramp of a veteran army that knew no defeat and now menaced both the State and National capitals. Neither the Confederates themselves nor their enemies knew the extent of their exhaustion nor of the accumulated strength of the Union army that occupied the position selected to decide the destiny of the Union.

Here the brave was to meet the brave. The love of home and country had brought to the front the citizen soldiery of Pennsylvania, and with a determination to fight and die, as only the brave will die, they met, with an heroic resistance, the surging columns that sought to sweep over them; but unable to stand the pressure of the first day, their lines wavered and nightfall found the Confederates victorious. Yet the inexhaustible resources of the Union enabled them to bring forward more reinforcements during the night, and as the Confederates had no reserve force to recruit from, the second day found them much weaker from the losses of the first day, while the second day found the enemy much stronger, which enabled them to reestablish the lost ground of the day previous and bid defiance to the further assaults of the invaders.

Their broken lines once reestablished with such an immense concentration of forces, their position was rendered impregnable; hence the most daring charge ever made by the Confederate army was met by the most deafening roar of artillery the combined armies of the world ever produced. The whole Element was a sheet of flame, the bursting shells sending their fragments in every direction, while the grape and canister united with the whizzing minnie ball in sweeping the field. Yet, amid all the combined powers of destruction that could be brought to bear by the ingenuity, skill and bravery of the great Union army, the Confederates did not turn their backs and flee for safety, but stubbornly held their ground and baffled every attempt to penetrate their lines until the close of day put an end to the raging conflict.

Though the army of Northern Virginia had not been routed, it had been repulsed and for the first time since its organization, had to acknowledge a defeat, and sullenly, reluctantly began during the night to fall back towards the

Potomac. Disheartened and dismayed, they felt that the Confederacy had received a dangerous, if not a fatal blow; and as the columns moved slowly along, leaving their dead and dying in the hands of the enemy, many and loud were the curses heaped upon those who had either straggled or been careless in the performance of duty. Many were the causes assigned for the failure—while the gallant LEE with his heart too generous to charge any one with the blame, exclaimed: "I alone am to blame." But officers and men could not charge any fault to their great and gallant commander, for they had been clamorous, as was the entire Southern populace, for the invasion that had resulted in defeat, and now that defeat had come they were clamorous for some cause to hold responsible for the defeat. They did not reflect that when valor meets valor, superior numbers must inevitably have their force. Neither did they reflect that the God of Battle sometimes allows valor crushed, and hence the inclination to "saddle" the responsibility of failure on some part of the gallant army that had heretofore known nothing but victory in a general conflict.

That gloomy despondent state of feeling pervaded the army when it returned to quarters in Virginia, and now a short rest was to be had; offenders must be punished and examples made that would be a warning in future. For this purpose, detachments were sent out to scour the whole country, and all who were absent without leave were brought in and dealt with. For the trial of such offences a court was organized, and to be arraigned before one of these courts was almost equivalent to conviction, for what proof can one who fell by the wayside, sick and footsore, produce to prove his innocence of any intention to shirk duty, except by his own statement? And of what avail is a statement of a private soldier before a military court?

It was before one of these courts that young Dickson was

arraigned, protesting his innocence of a crime the penalty of which was death. As we have before stated, he carried a surgeon's certificate which the surgeon said was a forgery; hence the charge of desertion. He was put upon trial, and the case turned on the evidence of an official whose veracity weighed against a private soldier whose life hung in suspence. The general court-martial decided against him and found him guilty and sentenced him "to be shot to death." The sentence of the court was approved by the higher authorities, and the day and hour of execution were fixed in an order that was read at dress parade to each Regiment of the Division. And with the reading of that order a cloud fell on the command.

The law was inexorable and the court had no alternative, and with a verdict of guilty the law prescribed punishment by death, without that saving clause which puts the offender at the mercy of the court, by allowing the words, "or other such punishment as the court may direct." But did he deserve death? Not a man in all the ranks believed it; they knew it was the letter of the law that was slaying him, but how to invoke its spirit, and whether the spirit could save him if it would, sorely puzzled them. They said if he should be punished at all it should be something less severe and irrevocable than death.

With that crushing weight the thought came home to their hearts that a good soldier and a true patriot was about to be shot for an example, and to satisfy a technicality of the stern military law.

They desired him to plead for pardon, but he scorned the asking for pardon, as it implied the acknowledgement of guilt. He would stand by the deed whatever the law called it, for he had sought no man's life, nor aimed a blow at the cause for which he had fought; if what he had done was a crime he could not help it. No matter if a thousand men were cowards he had not the blood of a poltroon in his veins—he would never touch his hat with head bowed low nor beg to have his name put on record as a pardoned deserter. His soul revolted at the very thought, and he would live and die by his solemn protest against that of guilt.

The sergeant and guard who guarded him by night offered him a chance of escape. "Fly for your life," said they. "Your innocent blood shall not rest on our hands. We will fire in the air and risk the chance of punishment for your escape." But he spurned the idea. Did ever the reluctant days drag a man to a more helpless and relentless doom?

If only he had fallen on some fierce field of battle, madly striking for his country! If only he had been slain on the skirmish line piloting the grand old army to victory! If he could have died in the hospital slowly wasted away by incurable wounds or disease, or been sacrificed in prison enduring torture or starvation with the fortitude born of honor and patriotism. If only in any way his blood might have been taken as a part of the price paid for liberty and freedom, all would have seemed well. But no, none of these; the very memory of his devotion to his country was to be blotted out, his record was to be blackened forever, and his name to become a legacy of shame to his children, and yet they knew he was conscious of no crime. Who could hold the cruel pen that was to write to the fond wife or mother the sad fate of their loved one? Who could apply the electric touch to the cold heartless wire* that would break the heart of loved ones who away at the south stood with eager and bated breath to watch the opening of the mails to receive information of an early return of the loved one, or his fall on the field of honor? Who could send home to her the picture of her own sweet face with the curl of hair on the glass, as he had worn it

*Telegraph message.

next to his heart so many years through blood and field, and write the words: "This, with his undying love, he bade me send you—his last request"?

Is it possible to save him in any way? was the query on all sides. Can he be pardoned or his sentence commuted? Yes, but only by petition through the Generals to the President. Would they sign it? Yes, we will get such a list of signatures that they will dare not refuse to sign it. This resolution being put in force, the signature of all the Lieutenants and Captains of the Brigade was affixed to the petition, and it was then sent to those commanding the Brigade, the Division, the Corps and thence to General Lee—all signed it and forwarded it to Richmond for the signature of the President. Would it be granted? Yes, all felt that the accused could not be shot, in the face of that list of names, yet an expression of anxiety lurked in every countenance.

A few days and no answer—some anxiety—solicitude increased—to-morrow, between the hours of 10 and 12 o'clock—oh, how terrible! Why this delay? The men lay in squads scattered through the camp, talking of the fateful day, until late in the night, none caring to sleep, the reveille seemed to arouse them from their first nap. The morning began to wear away and no answer yet. Oh, God! Why this delay? Is it fate? Why does everything move so slow when a human life is at stake? Will the driving wheels of the panting "iron horse" make their strokes more rapid this morning because of being freighted with the precious document, or will fate throw some obstacle in the way to prevent the arrival of the train in time to save his life?

What if the pardon is returned disapproved?

No, no! The President dare not refuse—such an act would be despotic! Low murmured threats of vengeance could be heard.

Nine o'clock—the train arrived—no pardon received. Alas! The last hope gone save one—would the Colonel stay the execution another day, or until the petition was returned? No, he feared the inexorable letter of military law—that law which knows no pity. The day and hour was appointed and the sacrifice must be made.

Ten o'clock—the drum sounded the stirring echoes of the "long roll" which signaled every man to "fall in," and no man could be excused. This was an example of warning, and all should witness the horrible deed. Another was to suffer the same fate—a young North Carolinian belonging to one of the North Carolina Brigades of the Division had been tried and sentenced for the same offence. As to his guilt or innocence we knew nothing—only knew that the scene was to be made doubly horrible by the taking of his young life.

The sunshine, the cloudless sky, the songs of birds and the roaring of the little "rapid Ann" river as its waters hastened on to the Rappahannock; the lonely and lofty peaks of the Blue Ridge in the background; the devastated plantations covered with camps, and this one the scene of a military execution; all these composed a never-to-be-forgotten picture. Down into the hearts of the whole Division it sank—photographed by the indelible feeling of awe as it made its impression forever.

At the tap of the drum all was bustle and commotion in camp—the drummer with mechanical precision rolled "sticks" as if by machinery, and there were no more questions asked.

From mere force of habit the men obeyed the summons, and in a few moments the Division was in motion. Silently, sullenly, the troops moved out into the main road; one Brigade after another, with the screds of their torn and tattered battle flags floating in the breeze. The hollow sound of the muffled drums, the silent tramp of the horror stricken men was so impressive that even the horses indicated something fearful hovered over the scene.

Regiment by Regiment filed into an open field in the center of which stood a lone persimmon tree; here a bank of red clay indicated the spot where the remains of the two unfortunate ones were to rest, and near by stood the posts to which they were to be pinioned to receive the fatal minnie balls into their hearts. Around this the troops were formed in hollow square leaving a small opening in the direction the executioners were to fire, and in this position they silently awaited the appearance of the solemn cortege.

Slowly down the road from the guard house it came—the guard and firing party with arms reversed, the prisoners with arms pinioned behind them, seated upon the coffin, mounted in a wagon drawn by four horses, with the sad-faced driver guiding them to the place of execution. Here they were assisted down from the wagon and marched along their Brigade to take a last leave of their comrades.

Roe Dickson as he passed around the lines scanned closely the features of the men until his gaze rested upon those with whom he had been most intimate and then pausing for a moment, said: "My friends, I die an innocent man, but I am going to a better world than this."

There was no more delay, everything was done quickly and with the utmost precision. Twelve men marched out and with faces flushed, halted in line and exchanged their guns for others that had been loaded for the occasion, six of which had balls and six with blank cartridge, thus leaving the men in merciful uncertainty, allowing each to think perhaps his was the harmless shot.

While the preliminaries were being arranged the most intense suspense prevailed and many wishful looks were cast in the direction of headquarters, hoping to catch the glimpse of a courier with the approved pardon. But Alas! Not so. Oh!

Why this indifference to precious human life? If our President loves his defenders why won't he send a special train and save the life of his humble subject and retain the confidence of his humble petitioners? Or if he has dispatched such a train, why won't the engineer put on every pound of steam and fly with lightning speed to the rescue of his fellow creature? Alas, how vain is hope when brought in contact with cruel fate!

The time for executions is at hand. The officer of the day read his warrant; drew the cap over the face of the prisoner; stepped back a little and amid the most awful silence, commanded:

"Attention! Rally!"

The clicking of those dozen locks was horrible; the victims stirred a little as if it was involuntarily; the air was stifling; the calm monotonous regularity of the commands was excruciating; the heartless business like manner was maddening.

Before the next command was given, Dickson exclaimed: "Boys, aim at my heart!" Then the command was: "Aim! Fire!"

There was a deafening crash—a cloud of smoke—a dull, heavy "thud"—and Dickson leaped forward severing the cord which he was pinioned with and fell a corpse. He was immediately turned upon his back and his clothes thrown back and the entire command marched in file to gaze through their blinding tears at the warm blood trickling from his bosom.

A glance at the ghastly wound with six balls in a circumference of that many inches proved that the firing party understood his last request.

The young North Carolinian sunk back a corpse with scarcely a convulsion, and thus ended the most sickening scene that has occurred since the eventful execution portrayed in the Sacred Scriptures, on which the sun refused to shine.

The bodies of the unfortunate ones were rudely consigned to the tomb, with no slab or stone to mark it from the ruder earth around—while in passing years, loving hands of a conquered but grateful people will decorate with flowers the last resting place of their fallen comrades whom fate had seen fit to consign to a more honored tomb. It is with a sad heart our mind often wanders to that lone grave, whenever the floral offering is annually being made,* and wonder if any kind hand ever places a flower where rests one who gave his life that army discipline might be preserved.

The men all having looked upon the corpse weltering in its gore, the march was again taken up, and to the sound of the drum, silently returned to camp. The day wore reluctantly away; the sun sank in a crimson horizon as if in harmony with the scene; and the evening shadows cast their gloom around as the peaks of the Blue Ridge shut out the orb of day; the dark vail of night shut out the scene—but the heart! Oh, how sick! Nothing to relieve it but nature's "sweet restorer" which soon stole over the entire camp, except the lone sentry who kept watch, while heroes slumbered.

Another day is ushered in, and with it the long looked for petition, and then from company to company sounded the news, Pardoned! But Alas! Too late! Too late! rang out through the camp, and a great excitement prevailed. Who is responsible for the sacrifice of that life? was the query on all sides. Was the paper held back by some designing officer who was determined that this man should die? Or was it negligence in the President? Whose blood shall we take in the

* Decoration Day—first celebrated in 1866.

next battle to avenge the blood of our comrade? Who is the proper one to do it? Thousands of other queries were propounded without any satisfactory answer, and the writer is inclined to take the more liberal view, and charge no man directly with this man's life, but charge it to the stern and cruel demands of war—the worst scourge that ever visited any nation and which breeds horrible events that no hand but the Omnipotent One can stay. May that Hand preserve our land from a recurrence of such scenes until the end of time.

IV

Confederate Women Subject of Praise

CAPT. W. F. SMITH BELIEVES MONUMENT SHOULD BE ERECTED TO THEIR MEMORY—PAYS TRIBUTE TO THE WOMEN OF THE CONFEDERACY.

This article is included primarily for the picture it gives of the young soldier—Albert or William—leaving home, and for William's theory of the drive behind the Southern patriot. It appeared in the Butts County Progress, *April 23, 1909 (Varner, p. 38).*

The campaign to honor Women of the Confederacy did not originate with William or with his brother Wilson. Newspapers throughout Georgia carried a supplement dated December 10, 1905, promoting action to recognize the Confederate Woman. Called Our Women In The War, *it was "a special edition in behalf of a monument to be erected in their honor."*

South Carolina was the first state to put up an official monument to women, and in Georgia there are commemorative markers or statues in Bibb, Lamar, McDuffie, Baldwin and Putnam Counties and perhaps others. Butts County did not subscribe to this idea, although like most counties it has a statue in memory of the Soldier, erected by the United Daughters of the Confederacy on the town square at Jackson in 1911.

EDITOR PROGRESS: Your paper of some weeks past was handed to me on sick-bed in McDonough.

I read a suggestion from my brother Wilson Smith on the Women of the Confederacy and I was forcibly impressed. I dare say there is hardly an ex-Confederate soldier in Butts county but what would vote to give the monument to the Women of the Confederacy instead of the Soldier, if the Daughters in Butts county decide to build one. And the new idea, the spinning wheel instead of the gun, is grand.

Yes, while other sections are raising the shaft in honor of the men who stood in line with gun and bayonet, let Butts county raise the shaft in honor and memory of the noble women who stood behind the lines and prayed and spun and wove, and buried the dead that were sent home. God bless them, heroines all. Who is it that went through that fearful ordeal that can now meditate upon the sacrifices, suffering and hardships of those mothers, wives, sisters and daughters and keep back the tears?

I can tell you what it was that caused the Confederate soldiers to astonish the world by their endurance of hardships and heroic bravery. It was the mother, wife, sweetheart and sister at home. And who has attempted to write the history of their heroic struggle? No one. And the half can never be told.

A personal explanation will illustrate the cause of the Confederate soldiers staying in the last ditch until killed or captured. Two years of the war had passed before I was old enough to go. My older brother as well as many neighbors had been brought home shot to pieces and many other dear friends left dead on the battle field. We knew then what it meant to go to the war. The time for my departure had come. My clothes were packed and I, a small boy,* had put on the

*According to muster record, 5ft. 7¾ in.

Confederate gray. My mother, with the tears all streaming down her cheeks, stood in the hall, at the foot of the stairs. Throwing her arms about my neck she said, "Put your trust in God and He will bring you through. I would rather you would die in battle than desert." And those were her last words of farewell.

Too full of emotion to utter one word, I left her with those words indelibly stamped on my conscience and memory. I was at once a man. From that moment I was a changed being.

In all the crack and onslaught of battle I did not stay there because I was brave but because my mother told me to. And I know that was the experience of thousands of others who suffered the pangs of hunger, cold and heat, shot and shell, sickness and death, on account of the loved ones at home.

They gave their sons, husbands, and brothers, lovers, all, and received back a fragment of battered and torn limbs, and they nursed them back into the greatest industrial struggle the world has ever known.

Yes, give the women the monument.

W. F. Smith, McDonough, Ga.

Notes

1. The Battalion William himself joined in Macon is not identifiable from current information. Many Confederate documents and records were destroyed to prevent their falling into Union hands, and the sketchiness of the account is partly a by-product of the South's Volunteer System. "Under this system, a body of men ranging in size from a company to a regiment or battery of artillery was raised locally by private enterprise and known as 'militia' . . . used principally for defense of the community." These groups were self-supporting and chose their own names (which frequently changed), officers, equipment and uniforms (Amann, p. v). Prior to battle the company then went to a state training camp—ten companies might be banded together as a regiment and mustered into active service (Robertson, p. 1).

2. Rose Hill Cemetery was begun in 1840 by Simri Rose (1708-1869), a Connecticut native, a newspaperman by profession, who helped plan, design, and build the city of Macon. (d'Antignac; Butler; White, p. 190).

3. Père la Chaise is a cemetery in Paris famed for its park-like hilly terrain, its trees, gardens, and statuary. Established by Napoleon in 1804 from earlier Royal Gardens and a Jesuit Retreat. *See Smithsonian,* November 1978 for pictures and commentary.

4. The area east of Macon, across the Ocmulgee River from Rose Hill, once concentrated the chief towns of the ancient Creek Indian Confederacy. The Creeks were removed to Oklahoma by the treaty of 1825 which had been signed at Indian Springs, near William's boyhood home.

5. It was not unheard of for a young lady to be wandering in the cemetery alone—Rose Hill was also a picnic spot with fountains, bandstand and park benches, as can be seen in the Rees Collection of old stereopticon pictures at the Washington Memorial Library in Macon. Anne Rose, youngest daughter of Simri Rose, (*see* note 2) left a diary of the war decade, her entry for January 9, 1861 reporting: "I have just taken a long walk in the cemetery, my first in months. I love always the quiet, thoughtful company of the dear place."

6. Normal field rations might have been only salty bacon and hardtack, but boxes from home and from friends like Florence's mother contained such treats as "good sorghum syrup . . . bread . . . pies, cakes . . . potatoes, onions and peppers . . . biscuits, rusks, broiled and fried chicken, ground coffee or blackberry wine" (Gay, pp. 47, 63). Or perhaps even "honey, sweet potatoes, sausages and some 'nise pork' " and in season, "watermelons, peaches, corn, grits, apple pies and cream and chicken fickens [fixings]" (Hagan, pp 3, 12).

7. *See* W. L. Fagan's collection of 1889. In his Introduction Fagan says: "The war songs of the South are a part of the history of the Lost Cause. They are necessary to the impartial historian in forming a correct estimate of the animus of the Southern people. Emotional literature is always a correct exponent of public sentiment, and these songs index the passionate sincerity of the South at the time they were written."

8. The Battle of Chickamauga occured September 19, 1863. This victory for the South was commended by General Lee in a dispatch dated September 24th:

GENERAL ORDERS, HDQRS. ARMY OF NORTHERN VIRGINIA,

NO. 89 *September* 24, 1863

The commanding general announces to the army, with profound gratitude to Almighty God, the victory achieved at Chickamauga by the army of General Braxton Bragg.

After a fierce and sanguinary conflict of two days, the Federal forces under General Rosecrans were driven, with heavy loss, from their strong positions, and, leaving their dead and wounded on the field, retreated under cover of night on Chattanooga, pursued by our cavalry.

Rendering to the Great Giver of Victory, as is most justly due, our praise and thanksgiving for this signal manifestation of His favor, let us extend to the army that has so nobly upheld the honor of our country the tribute of our admiration for its valor, and sympathy for its suffering and loss.

Invoking the continuous assistance of Heaven upon our efforts, let us resolve to emulate the heroic example of our brethren in the south, until the enemy shall be expelled from our borders and peace and independence be secured to our country.

[R. E. LEE,]
General.
(*Official Record,* Series I, vol. 29, p. 746)

9. This episode would have to have been in late February, as Andersonville Prison was not open before then. The prison was built to contain the overflow from crowded Belle Isle in Richmond (not captives from the active front) and the first inmates arrived before it was quite completed—only a few weeks before Albert left Macon forever. Thus the "loathsome reputation" described by William ten years later is evidently hindsight.

10. "With the interestingly individualistic military of the Confederates . . . a fight between a subordinate and his commanding officer did not necessarily mean a court martial" (McInvale to HaSk, 20 November 1977). It is not unlikely that civilian passengers were aboard trains carrying prisoners; there are accounts of Union prisoners describing this, but usually prisoners were loaded into freight, not passenger, cars.

11. The conscription question involved more than simply whether or not to draft. For instance, favors were given the conscripts, and the volunteers became resentful. Rebel John Hagan wrote home as early as July, 1862: "General merser has ishued an order

holding all the nonconscrips in sirvice 90 days after the experasion of their 12 months tirm, which has created a greateal of dissatisfatsin among the nonconscrips" (Hagan, p. 11).

12. Another soldier, Joel Arthur Walker, of Company K, left a brief record of the 45th Georgia Regiment now on file at the Georgia Department of Archives and History: "The Army of Northern Virginia . . . remained in Winter Quarters or rather 'Spring Quarters' until the 4th of May. During our stay at this place the regiment was put in an admirable condition by the energy & perseverance of the commanding officer. Drilling was the order of the day and at the time above mentioned it was 425 strong, with a morale not to be surpassed. Time passed—speculations as to what the summer months would reveal were rife and varied."

13. Card playing was a favorite pastime of Yanks or Rebs alike, in camp, but "fearful of an angry God, soldiers usually discarded such instruments of sin before entering battle" (Price, p. 25).

14. This ingenuity displayed by soldiers in camp might have been what earned them the name "doughboys," a name by which infantrymen were called as early as the Civil War (Aikman). Necessity mothered still other inventions, other places. One soldier wrote: "I am writing by [the light of] a piece of rope in a sardine box filled with tallow, an invention of my own and now the whole regiment has them" (Yow).

15. The battle around Lynchburg occurred June 17 and 18, 1864. This city contained seventeen major hospital facilities, and as a supply center was second only to Richmond in importance, for Virginia. Through it passed eight railroads and a canal; without this transportation system in operation Richmond would fall (Gerhardt). General Hunter thus organized a major attack, but lack of ammunition forced him to turn west. Thirteen hundred convalescents from Lynchburg hospitals participated in General Early's repulsion of the Federal troops.

16. General Benjamin Franklin Butler became bottled up in a loop in the James River and tried to cut a canal through. The Union General was known as "Beast" because of his personality, temper, and undiplomatic manner.

17. The fort historically known as "Fort Hell" was Union-held *Sedgwick,* only 500 yards from Rebel Fort Mahone, called "Fort Damnation." However, William's "Fort Hell" seems to be enemy battery #4, adjacent to *Fort Stedman,* which was closer to and therefore more likely to be damaging to Pocahontas and the gas works.

18. A fellow soldier, Hugh Neisler of Butler, Georgia, in Company E of William's Regiment (45th Ga.) wrote to William in 1902, responding to an article William had published (as yet unlocated) on the Battle of the Wilderness. He was with the regiment when William, having recovered from his wounds, joined them at Fort Clifton—a semi-permanent work between Swift Creek and the Appomattox River in present day Colonial Heights. Of this period Neisler wrote: "I remember Geo Gunn of Co. I is he living? I remember when we [were] on swift creek below Petersburg he was with the Pioneer corps. one day he came over to see his co, in going back to his camp he came upon some men butchering a beef they gave him some of the beef he carried it to his camp. The beef being found in his possession he was courtmartialed, found guilty, and his sentence was to go back to ranks and to carry a log of wood weighing so many lbs for 18 days. but was told that the sentence would be commuted if he would tell who killed the beef. (He said during the courtmartial that he did not kill it) He would not tell but went back to his co and carried the log of wood every evening till his time was out . . . I always thought he did right."

19. Trench warfare had its beginnings in the siege of Petersburg, later developed to its fullest in World War I, at which time the Petersburg area was used as a training ground (Meade Station Trail pamphlet). "For the soldiers of both armies it was 10 months of

rifle bullets, artillery and mortar shells, relieved only by rear area tedium: drill and more drill, salt pork and corn meal, burned beans and bad coffee . . . sloshing mire and steaming trenches in summer . . . ice and snow and mud in winter . . ." (Petersburg pamphlet).

20. There is no evidence or proof that Florence was other than an imaginary heroine. Yet Simri Rose's daughter Leila (*see* notes 2 and 5) died in Macon of typhoid fever at age seventeen, and was buried July 29, 1865 in the family plot in Rose Hill Cemetery, overlooking the Ocmulgee River. On June 8, her sister Anne had written in her diary, "Leila my darling sister is sick. I am afraid she is going to be very ill." We do not know, in actual fact, whether William knew the Rose family, but Leila must have been typical of the genteel young Southern lady represented by Florence, in death as well as in life. Her obituary, in the *Macon Telegraph and Confederate* (5 August 1865), is characteristic of the period:

OBITUARY
LEILA F. ROSE

"Gather the rose buds while ye may,
For time is every flying;
The lovely flower that blooms to-day
To-morrow shall be dying."

How forcibly are we reminded of the truth of the above thought, by the early and untimely death of our young friend. . . . The calm dignity, the eminent social qualities, the urbanity of our young friend had gathered around her a large circle of associates, who appreciated the pleasures of her society.

Three years ago she felt the importance of seeking more enduring pleasures than could be obtained in the fitful enjoyments of the world. She sought the peace of heart which comes from above, the gift of grace, the value of which is seemingly enhanced by a consciousness of moral and religious rectitude. . . . Under the impulses of her vivacious young nature, the peculiar temptations of the times, and the influence of young companions she, like thousands of others . . . wavered for a time, but soon saw and felt her folly and abandoned it. . . .

Her many good qualities of mind and heart did fair to develop a true, noble and useful woman, and constitute her an ornament of the church, but at the early age of seventeen years, she has been called to a seat in the upper sanctuary. She died in the calm and full assurance of her acceptance with God through the merits of His Son.

"Early, bright, transient, chaste as morning dew,
She sparkled, was exhaled and went to heaven."

21. William's grandson, Howard Linch, gives one account of William's capture: ". . . he told me that he was captured by a Maryland regiment and that one of them said come on Johnnie we won't hurt you. A Yankee Sergeant detached himself from the action to escort the prisoner to the rear. The Sergeant took his knife and cut the straps on Smith's haversack, saying, you won't be needing that any more. At this point they came under the fire of a Confederate Battery, and one of the prisoners was hit in the shoulder by a ball that was skipping along the ground. Encouraged by the Yankee's example and his admonition 'run Johnnie run' their flight was more precipitated than dignified." (Letter to aunts, 3 February 1961). Hugh Neisler (*see* note 18) wrote: "I was taken prisoner 25th of March the evening we were sent out to recapture our picket line (you remember the 35th & 45th of our Brigade were sent) There was 116 of our Regt at Point Lookout [where] we arrived . . . 28th of March." A detailed account of this battle and a list of the casulaties, including the name of "cpl. W. F. Smith" appeared in the *Macon Telegraph and Confederate,* Thursday, 19 April 1865.

22. Point Lookout was a large Federal Prison in Maryland located where the Potomac runs into the Chesapeake Bay, which was undoubtedly the "ocean" to Albert's inland eyes. Point Lookout was established in August of 1863 with no barracks, the prisoners, all enlisted men, living in tents (Hemmerlein). It is a pity William did not record any of the many jests and "quaint sayings

of Sergeant Jake and Corporal Dick," but another inmate did. John Omenhausser kept a sketchbook of cartoons illustrating the ingenuity and spiritedness of the captives despite their hard lot. This brilliant record has been reprinted in a history of Point Lookout by Edwin Beitzel, 1972. The prison "was a horrible place with a death rate higher than Andersonville" (Letter to HaSk, 31 October 1977). Another Georgian, the Macon poet Sidney Lanier, was also at Point Lookout (November 1863-March 1864) and began his first novel, *Tiger Lilies,* at this same place.

23. What William may have meant by "fanatical spirit" may be revealed in some of his unpublished writings of several decades later, ("Cause and Effect", ca. 1900): "While the patriotic liberty loving class of all sections were engaged in the deathly struggle during the civil war, there was a money loving class, who cared more for money than for God or Government who speculated on the necessities of the Government and the misfortunes of the people. And so, when the war was ended they had ample means to take advantage of the chaotic condition of public sentiment, and the demoralized condition of the Government, and so shape legislation as to make themselves forever the masters of the liberties of the people. The great Union armies returned to their homes, terribly chastened but elated with their dearly bought victory. They turned to the pursuit of developing their resources, caring nothing for legislation or political affairs. The fragments of the Southen armies returned home feeling they had been overwhelmed and ruined. They turned to the problem of keeping from starving, caring nothing for legislation. And so, while the great mass of the people, both North and South, were engaged in the laudable work of making a living and rebuilding the waste places, the speculating class fastened upon the Nation a system of class legislation that the masses could never remove and which finally led to the downfall of the Republic."

24. Some prisoners escaped the rigors of captivity by taking the Oath of Allegiance to the United States soon after their capture.

Most stuck it out to the bitter end, however, and after the surrender, most Rebels acknowledged their defeat with grace and dignity, complying with the Oath in deed as well as word, despite their bitter disappointment in the outcome of the war. Those who took the Oath prior to Lee's surrender at Appomattox were not easily forgiven by the men who held out, nor by their heirs, even to the present day in some instances. However, Beitzell says there was much in the way of mitigating circumstances: "the men in these prison camps had a hard time of it and should not be judged harshly" (Letter to HaSk, 31 October 1977). William's Oath of Allegiance, signed on his separation from Point Lookout June 19, 1865, identifies him as being 5 foot, 7¾ inches tall, dark-haired, and dark-complexioned, with eyes of grey.

25. Sources for this sketch were letters and notes from Jewell Smith, newspaper clippings in the Varner and Hattie Smith scrapbooks and loaned by relatives, primarily the Bicentennial edition of the *Jackson Progress-Argus*, also Howard Linch notes, and Echols, Ellis, Settle, Scruggs, Johnson, Lane, and others listed in the Bibliography.

26. The white settlers of Butts County lived peaceably with their Indian neighbors and could probably have continued to do so. But as state policy, the natives were seen as a threat to westward expansion. In 1825 Georgia finally managed to get the treaty signed by which most of the Lower Creek nation's lands in Georgia were exchanged for lands across the Mississippi. On February 12 of that year the transaction was made in what was later called the Varner house at Indian Springs—an inn built by William McIntosh, half-breed chief of the Lower Creeks. Here McIntosh and other chiefs signed the Second Treaty of Indian Spring, giving up their last Georgia land. The action was repudiated by most of his people as involving the vested interest and personal motive of only a few. Hopothleoholo, orator of the Alabama Creeks, denounced the signers in a speech delivered from a boulder near the McIntosh House, and McIntosh himself was executed by a band of Warriors

at his home in Carroll County the following April (*see* Suddeth, p. 148 for traditional white slant; Mooney, p. 224 for native point of view; also Georgia Historical Marker at the site.)

27. Samuel Kirby Smith, "County History Important Work," *Jackson Progress-Argus*, 21 March 1930. Kirby Smith (1866–1945) was William's younger brother, born the year after the war and named for the Confederate General of the same name.

28. The name of "W. F. Smith, *Middle Georgia Argus,*" appears in a list of delegates to the Georgia Press Association convention, in *The Gainesville Eagle*, 20 May 1878.

29. Most of Aney Smith's poems and papers have been lost, but one is remembered by her granddaughter Ethel Smith of Jackson, Georgia, daughter of William's brother Jack: "Sisters, sisters, do not fuss and frown,/You know the day will come when one will be sad/And the other put in the grown [ground]."

30. "Camp Meeting" was and is an out-of-doors season of revival and praise originally coinciding with the laying-by time in late summer between planting and harvest. Its beginnings were strongly influenced, in the American rural church, by Indian traditions of ceremonial thanksgiving and feasting, and it may even have had its origins in the idea of the Biblical Feast of Booths, or Tabernacles, in Leviticus 23:39–43 (Anthropology Department, Georgia State University for a study of Tent Meetings today).

31. Miss Jo Varner's father, Edward, bought the McIntosh hotel soon after it was built and it was later called the Varner house, until it became a museum in recent years and is known once again as the McIntosh House. Miss Jo lived there until her death in 1928, at the age of 92. The house still contains the desk on which the Indian Treaty of 1825 was signed. Making scrapbooks for shut-ins, spelling-bee prizes, and gifts, was a hobby of Miss Jo's.

Several of these are on file at the Georgia Department of Archives and History, along with some of her prolific correspondence (S. L. Thompson, "Three Remarkable Women Noted for Longevity," *Jackson Progress-Argus*, ca. 1930).

32. A Romulus Dixon and a Cicero Dickerson were both among William's acquaintances. Dickerson (Co. I, 45th Ga.) was "retired to invalid corps April 10, 1864." Dixon (14th Ga.) was courtmartialed September, 1863 under General Orders #88 of June 24 (O. R., Series IV, vol. 2, pp. 607–8). But as early as February of that year, notices were appearing in the Confederate press offering $30.00 a head for apprehension and delivery of specific men at large. One such notice was signed by the Captain Folsom mentioned herein (*Atlanta Southern-Confederate*, 4 February 1863, Ga. Archives Regimental Files). A report of the 14th Ga. Regiment in Winter Quarters near Fredericksburg appeared on p. 1 of the *Macon Daily Telegraph* 25 August 1863.

Acknowledgments

My sincere thanks and appreciation to:

Barbara Story, Morton McInvale, members of the Rose family and others for information on Macon and Rose Hill;

The Georgia Department of Archives and History for permission to quote certain unpublished matter;

The National Archives and Records Service, Cartographic Branch, Washington, D. C. for aid in locating old maps;

Representatives of the National Park Service—Mr. Wallace Elms of Petersburg, Mr. John Flister of Andersonville, Mr. Dennis Kelly of Manassas—and Mr. Thomas G. Ledford of the Lynchburg Museum System for supportive documents;

Dr. Bell I. Wiley for guidance on specific questions;

Mr. Kim Holien, Historian of the War Department, Washington, D. C. and Mr. Edwin Beitzell of Abell, Maryland, for corroboration on prison camps;

Friends and relatives who have shared generously their time, information and materials;

My family for their interest and assistance along the way.

HaSk

Main Events

September 16, 1845	William Ferguson Smith born.
April 12, 1861	War began at Fort Sumter, S. C.
July 1, 1863	Battle of Gettysburg, Pa.
September, 1863	WFS joined volunteer battalion, Macon, Ga.
September 19, 1863	Battle of Chickamauga, Tenn.
March 15, 1864	WFS enlisted in regular army, Jackson, Ga.
March 22, 1864	Mustered in, camp near Orange Court House, Va.
May 6, 1864	Wounded at Battle of the Wilderness, Va.
June 17, 1864	Battle around Lynchburg, Va.
July, 1864	WFS re-joined regiment at Petersburg, Va.
July 20, 1864	Battle of Peachtree Creek, Atlanta, (Sam Smith).
July 30, 1864	Battle of the Crater, Petersburg, Va.
November 10, 1864	WFS promoted to Corporal.
November 17, 1864	Sherman's Army invaded Butts County, Ga.
March 25, 1865	WFS captured at Petersburg, Va.

April 9, 1865	Lee surrendered at Appomattox, Va.
April 14, 1865	Lincoln shot.
June 19, 1865	WFS released from Point Lookout Prison, Md.
December 24, 1867	Married Mary Talitha Preston, Flovilla, Ga.
1876	Elected Captain of local militia unit; Sam Smith elected to Ga. legislature.
1877	Bought *Indian Springs Echo*; started *Butts County* (Later *Middle Ga.*) *Argus*; published *The Rival Lovers*, serially.
1880	Published additional chapters, about Roe Dickson.
1882	Southern Railway entered Butts Co.
March 2, 1887	Mary Talitha died.
1888	Flovilla and Indian Springs Railway began (to 1918).
1889	WFS selected site and helped build Indian Springs Campground.
October 23, 1890	Married Martha Elizabeth Mitchell.
1893	Began *Flovilla-Indian Springs Enterprise*; 1894, *National Headlight*; 1899 *Headlight-Homeseeker*.
February 23, 1911	Lloyd Shoals (Jackson) dam first in operation.
March 16, 1912	William Ferguson Smith died.

Bibliography

Some further references of interest on the period, literature, and locale.

Aaron, Daniel. *The Unwritten War: American Writers and the Civil War.* Civil War Centennial Commission Series. New York: Alfred A. Knopf, 1973.

Aikman. *See* Bellard.

Amann, William Frayne, ed. *Personnel of the Civil War.* New York: Thomas Yoseloff, 1961.

Anderson, Eugene. "Interesting Civilization Flourished at Smith's Mill." Clipping from the *Macon Telegraph*, n.d.

Andersonville: National Historic Site, Georgia. Pamphlet of the National Park Service, U.S. Department of the Interior, 1975.

Ball, Alice Morton. *Compounding in the English Language.* New York: H. W. Wilson Co., 1941. A historical study of changing styles in hyphenating and word formation.

Beitzell, Edwin W. *Point Lookout Prison Camp for Confederates.* Abell, Maryland: St. Mary's County, 1972. Contains reproductions of John Omenhausser's contemporary sketches.

———. Letters to HaSk.

Bellard, Alfred. *Gone for a Soldier.* Boston: Little, Brown and Co., 1975. Reviewed by Leo Aikman, "Ready on the Home Front." *Atlanta Constitution*, 18 January 1978, editorial page.

Boatner, Mark Mayo III. *Civil War Dictionary.* New York: David McKay, 1959.

Burgess, Robert H. Mariner's Museum, Newport News, Virginia. Letter to HaSk, 21 October 1977. Information on the Steamer Keyport and other prison ships.

Butler, John C. *Historical Record of Macon and Central Georgia.* Macon: J. W. Burke Co., 1879. Reprinted by Macon Historical Society by permission of the Colonial Dames, 1961.

Butts County, Georgia, 1825–1976, History of. Compiled by Lois McMichael for the William McIntosh Chapter, Daughters of the American Revolution in Jackson, Georgia. Atlanta: Cherokee Publishing Co., 1978.

Buzzette, Isabel and Frank McKenney. Information on Confederate Monuments in Georgia. Conversations with HaSk, 1978.

Cox, Jacob D. *Campaigns of the Civil War,* vol. 10, *The March to the Sea.* New York: Charles Scribners Sons, 1882.

d'Antignac, Munroe. "Simri Rose: Macon Pioneer." *Macon Telegraph,* 31 January 1943.

DeRoche, Louis. "The Novel of the Civil War." Unpublished Thesis. Mimeographed. Athens: University of Georgia, 1936. *See also* William Hammack, "Back to Athens Town," *Atlanta Journal and Constitution Magazine,* 10 June 1973, p. 34, for an interview with DeRoche.

Derry, Joseph Tyrone. *Story of the Confederate States.* Richmond: B. F. Johnson Publishing Co., 1895.

Echols, Samuel A. *General Assembly of 1878: Biographical Sketches.* Pp. 225–226. Atlanta: James P. Harrison and Co., 1878.

Ellis, Clara Thompson. "A Bit of Jasper County History." *Monticello* (Georgia) *News,* 3 March 1966.

———. Various clippings from *Monticello News,* n.d.

———. Manuscript. Notes and history of the Thompson and Smith families.

Fagan, W. L., ed. *Southern War Songs.* New York: M. T. Richardson and Co., 1890.

"Fashion Fads." *Atlanta Journal,* 26 March 1910. Anderson Collection, Atlanta Historical Society files.

Gay, Mary A. H. *Life in Dixie During the War.* With an introduction by Joel Chandler Harris. *Atlanta Constitution* Job Office, 1892. New edition, Decatur: DeKalb Historical Society, 1979.

Gerhardt, E. Alvin, Jr. "The Battle of Lynchburg, June 17–18, 1864." *Lynchburg Historical Society & Museum Bulletin,* vol. 3, no. 3. Lynchburg, Virginia, n.d.

Gilham, William. *Manual of Instruction for the Volunteers and Militia of the Confederate States.* Richmond: West and Johnson, 1861.

Hagan, John W., Confederate Letters of. Edited by Bell Irvin Wiley. Athens: University of Georgia Press, 1954.

Hardeman, Capt. Jno. "From the Trenches Near Petersburg, Va." *The Telegraph and Confederate,* Macon, Georgia, 19 April 1865. A full and first-hand report of the battle in which WFS was taken captive.

Harvey, John. "Bicentennial Bits." Series in *Monticello* (Georgia) *News*, 1975–1976.

Harwell, Richard S. *Confederate Music.* Chapel Hill: University of North Carolina Press, 1950.

Henderson, Lillian. *Roster of the Confederate Soldiers of Georgia, 1861–1865.* State of Georgia: Longino and Parker, 1960.

Hemmerlein, Richard F. *Prisons and Prisoners of the Civil War.* Boston: Christopher Publishing House, 1934.

Hermann, Isaac. *Memoirs of a Confederate Veteran* (1911). Lakemont, Georgia: CSA Press, 1974.

Jackson Progress-Argus. Jackson, Georgia. Various clippings and articles through the years, especially the Bicentennial Edition, 1 July 1976.

Johnson, Dr. Z. T. *The Story of Indian Springs Holiness Camp.* Wilmore, Kentucky: Asbury College, 1965.

Jones, Doyle, Jr. "It's This Way." *Jackson Progress-Argus,* 29 November 1973.

Jones, Vincent. "The Last Straw." *Jackson Progress-Argus,* 22 April 1976.

Lane, Rosa. "Sketches of Two Early Patriots." *Jackson Progress-Argus,* 12 September 1935.

Linch, Eugenia. Manuscript. Notes and reminiscences of WFS.

Linch, Howard. Letter to Alice Thompson, et. al. 3 February 1961. Details of WFS military record.

Lindsey, Robert Parham. "Reminiscences." Private Papers in the Civil War Regimental Files. Georgia Department of Archives and History, Atlanta.

Lively, Robert A. *Fiction Fights the Civil War: An Unfinished Chapter in the Literary History of the American People.* Chapel Hill: The University of North Carolina Press, 1957.

Macon Heritage Tour. Pamphlet of the Greater Macon Chamber of Commerce.

Meade Station Trail. Pamphlet of the Petersburg National Battlefield Area. National Park Service. U. S. Department of the Interior.

Mooney, James. *Historical Sketch of the Cherokee.* A Smithsonian Institution Press Book. Chicago: Aldine Publishing Co., 1975.

McInvale, Morton. "Macon and the Civil War." *Macon Telegraph and News.* Section VI, Sesquicentennial Edition, 28 September 1973.

———. Letters to HaSk, 1977-1978.

———. Unpublished Thesis. Tallahassee: Florida State University, 1973. Mimeographed copy at Georgia Department of Archives and History, Atlanta.

Official Record. See War of the Rebellion.

Palmer, Prentice. " 'Gray Ladies' ". *Atlanta Journal and Constitution.* 4 December 1977. An interview with Georgia's seven surviving Civil War Widows.

Petersburg National Battlefield. Pamphlet of the National Park Service. U. S. Department of the Interior.

Price, William H. *Civil War Handbook.* Civil War Research Associates Series. Fairfax, Virginia: Prince Lithograph, 1961.

Richmond. Pamphlet of the National Park Service. U. S. Department of the Interior.

Robertson, James I., Jr. *The Civil War.* Washington, D. C.: U. S. Civil War Centennial Commission, 1963.

Rose, Anne. "Diary." Typescript copy. Private Papers on file at Wesleyan College, Macon; The Southern Historical Collection at the University of North Carolina, Chapel Hill; and Georgia Department of Archives and History, Atlanta.

Salter, Charles. "Group Hopes to Make Smith's Mill State Park." Georgia Rambler Column. *Atlanta Journal,* 12 August 1976.

Schairer Collection. Microfilm. Georgia Department of Archives and History, Atlanta. Deeds, letters, etc., donated by Marjorie Thomas Schairer, a granddaughter of WFS.

Scruggs, Carroll P. *Georgia Historical Markers.* Helen, Georgia: Bay Tree Grove, 1973.

Settle, John Blackman. "William Ferguson Smith." Winning essay for Butts County in a contest for students on "The Citizen (Living or Dead) of My County Who Has Made the Greatest Contribution to the State of Georgia." Sponsored by Rich's, Inc., of Atlanta on its Diamond Jubilee, 1942. Printed in the *Manchester* (Georgia) *Mercury,* n.d.

Smith, Hattie (Harriet Ann). Scrapbook in the possession of HaSk. Contains primarily obituaries, columns, personal writings.

Smith, Jewell Gem. Notes on WFS and letters to HaSk.

Smith, Rebecca W., "Catalogue of the Chief Novels and Short Stories by American Authors Dealing with the Civil War and Its Effects, 1861-1899." *Bulletin of Bibliography,* vol. 16 (1939) pp. 193-194 and vol. 17 (1940) pp. 10 ff.

Stewart, Francis E. "Jasper County Indian Trails." *Monticello* (Georgia) *News,* n.d. Includes reference to an article on the Oakfuskee Trail in the *Georgia Historical Quarterly,* vol. 30, March 1955.

Stonewall Songbook. Richmond: West and Johnson, 1864 and 1865. Copy in Emory University Music Collection.

Suddeth, Ruth Elgin, Isa Lloyd Osterhout and George Lewis Hutcheson. *Empire Builders of Georgia.* Austin, Texas: The Steck Co., 1951.

Varner, Jo. Scrapbook of clippings made for WFS, 1912.

Walker, Joel Arthur. "Report." Private papers in the Civil War Regimental Files. Georgia Department of Archives and History, Atlanta.

Wallace, Julia. "People Explore Macon Cemetery." *Atlanta Journal and Constitution,* 4 September 1977.

Wallace, Robert. "The Elegies and Enigmas of Romantic Père-Lachaise." *Smithsonian,* November 1978.

The War of the Rebellion: A Compilation of the Official Records of the Union and Confederate Armies. Washington, D. C., 1900. *See also Atlas* of the Official Records. New York: Thomas Yoseloff, 1958.

White, George. *Historical Collections of Georgia.* New York, 1854.

———. *Statistics of the State of Georgia.* Savannah, 1848.

Wiley, Bell Irvin. *The Life of Johnny Reb.* New York: Doubleday and Co., 1943 and 1971.

Yow, Thomas Anderson (Company H, 15th Georgia Regiment). Letter to Elizabeth Dean from Camp Walker, Southern Army of the Potomac, 1 September 1861. Copy in possession of Stovall family, Lavonia, Georgia.